BLOODY MARY

BLOODY MARY

AND OTHER TALES
FOR A DARK NIGHT

STEFAN DZIEMIANOWICZ

**BARNES
& NOBLE
BOOKS**

NEW YORK

2000 Barnes & Noble Books

ISBN 0-7607-2041-X *casebound*
ISBN 0-7607-2040-1 *paperback*

Printed and bound in the United States of America

04 MC 9 8 7
00 01 02 03 04 MP 9 8 7 6 5 4 3 2 1

BVG

FOR MY MOTHER AND FATHER,
WHO ALWAYS TELL GREAT STORIES

Contents

Introduction   ix

Tall Tales for the Campfire

Campfire Story   5
Initiation into Terror   11
Funhouse of Fear   17
Body Snatched   25
The Summer of Cropsey   31

Tales for After Dinner

The Doom of the House of Gaskell   45
Secret Ingredient   51
Just Desserts   55

Urban Legends

Brainy Type   65
Cocoon   69
Mule   75
Coat Carrier   81
The Giving Kind   87
Crazy Sally   91

Slumber Party Terrors

Don't Turn on the Light!   97
Final Call   103
Why the Doctor Went Mad   111
Ginger Snaps   117

Short Shivers for Long Car Rides

Stay Away from Wilson Drive!   127
Backseat Driver   133
One More   141
Death Takes Its Toll   147
Roadside Stop   151
Hook Ending   155

Frights for the Christmas Fireside

He Sees You When You're Sleeping   163
Yule Love Him   169
O Christmas Tree!   173
. . . In Small Packages   179
Hearth of Horror   185

Halloween Horrors

Tricks and Treats   197
Masquerade   203
Scarecrow   207
Sweets to the Sweet   215
Bloody Mary   219

Introduction

I've got a strange story to tell you.

It's about something that happened to me when I was sixteen. Though many years have passed, the details are still as vivid in my mind as though it had happened just yesterday.

It was a winter evening, and the farm I grew up on just south of the Catskill Mountains was blanketed with five inches of snow from flurries the day before. The sun was just beginning to dip below the hills to the west. The air was crisp and cold and seemed to amplify the far-off sounds of gunshots from hunters walking the ridge above our land. The sky had that hazy red glow so typical of rural winter skies. It was still fairly light out—I can't stress that enough—but it was that eerie time of year when the shadows cast in the twilight looked dark and impenetrable from only a few feet away.

My thirteen-year-old brother, Richard, and my sister, Ginny, were getting ready to head into town for an evening basketball game being played at our high school. I was firing the ignition of my folks' car, which I'd been given permission to drive. Ginny, who had slid into the passenger seat next to me, was putting on her seat belt. Richard, ever the gentleman, had just shut Ginny's door for her and was circling around behind the car to get into the backseat on my side, the backdoor lock on Ginny's side having been broken over a year before.

I had just adjusted the rearview mirror. It had to be moved, along with the seat, from the position my slightly taller father had put them in. Richard's image entered the mirror but disappeared into one of the car's blind spots as he maneuvered around the back. I chose that moment to look down at the gas gauge and make sure we had enough to get us into the town. The tank was half-full.

I was waiting for Richard to open the backdoor. He seemed to be taking his time. After about half a minute I turned my head around to see what was going on.

There was no sign of Richard.

I looked over at our house, which sat atop a slight rise maybe twenty yards away from the passenger side of the car. Richard could be as forgetful as any other little brother and often had to run back to the house to get something just as we were getting ready to pull out of the driveway. But I didn't see him there, and there was no way he could have covered the distance to the house in so short a time, even if he'd sprinted.

I looked in the other direction, off toward the fields that stretched away from the driver's side of the car toward the west. There was still enough sunlight to see a solid blanket of white snow, unbroken by footprints.

I told Ginny to sit tight as I slipped out of my shoulder harness. All I could think about was how hard I was going to throttle my little brother if his prank made us miss the opening tip-off.

I don't know what I was expecting to see when I got behind the car. Maybe I thought I'd see Richard ducking down behind the car as a joke, or possibly discover he'd fallen in the snow and was hurt. But he wasn't there.

I ran back to the house to get my parents only after I looked into the shadow the car made on the ground behind it. Richard's footsteps led up to the shadow, then abruptly stopped. I saw the imprint of his left and right boots leading up to the shadow, which was exactly where he'd walked into the blind spot of the rearview mirror. There was a left footprint stepping into the shadow, but no right print. The snow around them was completely untouched.

From all visible signs, my brother seemed to have vanished into thin air—in mid-stride.

My parents called the local sheriff. It took him and his deputies twenty minutes to get out to our farm, and by that time the night was pitch black. They staked out the area where Richard had last been seen. They called in forensics teams to analyze every square inch of snow-covered ground leading up to and around the car. They thought about calling the medical examiner but decided you only did that when you had a body to show.

I don't know how much they believed anything I told them. My family never knew what the police really thought had happened. They ran a notice in the paper and put up posters in the post offices throughout the state. They started a missing persons file for Richard that supposedly stayed open for a full seven years.

But we never saw my brother again.

The next spring, I noticed something peculiar. The place where we parked our car was not a paved driveway. It was just a patch of pasture where driving back and forth had flattened the grass down into ruts. There was a small circle of grass just behind the car that was completely browned out—which made no sense, since it had been a rainy spring.

I knew what that circle corresponded to.

We dug into the ground for several feet, hoping that we might find something—anything—that would give us a clue about Richard. But we never did. Efforts to reseed the ground after we filled the hole back in were useless. To this day, my parents' farm still has a circle of barren ground that won't support grass, or plants, or even weeds.

My parents haven't been the same since that winter Richard disappeared. That's probably why I've never told them what I'm about to share with you. I first noticed it on a winter's evening about five years later. I was home for a visit, smoking a cigarette out by my car, when the wind came whipping down the hill from our house. It was just hard enough to make a noise as it whistled around the branches of the trees overhead and through the dead weeds on the ground. And in the lonely, far-off noise it made I swore I could hear a voice.

It was Richard's—crying, pleading.

Then it faded away.

I've heard it many winters since. I'm now a man of forty-two. But the voice I hear is still that of a terrified thirteen-year-old boy, lost somewhere and trying to find his way home.

There's a few things you should know about the story I've just told you.

I didn't grow up on a farm.

I never had a sister or a younger brother.

And the story itself is a favorite of campire and fireside storytellings, tucked here and tweaked there to give it the authoritative sound of a weird personal experience.

I first heard a version of this story when I was a kid. Probably around a fire at Scout camp, maybe at a story-telling session around the Christmas hearth. At the time, I thought it one of the scariest stories I had ever heard.

Many years later, I ran across a plot summary for the story in a book of so-called strange-but-true phenomena. There was no mistaking the brief account of a boy who vanished mysteriously as he walked around a horse in an open field and was never seen again; it was the germ of the disappearing brother story that had haunted me since childhood. But I found the story in the book disappointing. It was related as one of several examples of inexplicable disappearances recorded over the centuries. The flat, serious prose of the writer, whose job it was simply to report the story, lacked the drama and the pathos that had made the version told to me so disturbing.

I realized, then, that the person who had told me that story so many years ago might well have read the same book as I—and that he might have thought the same thing I did about this unforgivably bland account of a creepy encounter with the unknown:

There's the makings of a good horror tale in that story.

The stories in *Bloody Mary* are horror tales, but not just any horror tales. Each one of them is based on a weird theme or idea not unlike the tale of the vanishing brother. Many draw their inspiration from urban legends, those reports of bizarre injuries and near- (or much too closer than near-) brushes with death that happen so often to friends of friends you almost can't believe they've never once happened to you. Some take their cue from actual stories I remember hearing around the fire, or from friends who relayed them to me after hearing them from someone else. A few spring from basic superstitions or the kind of oddball received wisdom that gets heads nodding in agreement when it's mentioned in uncritical company. I'm sure you've heard some of them—but I'll bet you haven't heard them all.

In each instance, I have tried to be mindful of the basic principles that made that fireside story so effective so many years before: the use of credible characters and settings; the gradual buildup to a final horror.

My hope is that these stories will not just be effective for the solitary reader curled up with the book on a dark night, but lend themselves to reading out loud to others. They're short and to the point. And they have been grouped into a variety of categories defined by seasons or settings where storytelling often takes place: after dinner, on Halloween, around the fireplace at Christmas, and so on. In each case, they are preceded or followed by an account of the legend that inspired them.

My task is fulfilled if these stories give you the same kind of shivers I experienced when I heard similar tales of terror as a young boy.

By all means, then, why don't you all draw a bit closer toward the fire. It's warm, and safe, and its light dispels a good many things you might not want to see anyway.

I've got some strange stories to tell you.

Tall Tales for the Campfire

Campfire tales are among the oldest story types in the oral tradition. Indeed, it's generally assumed that the campfire tale was invented not too long after man discovered fire.

The earliest campfire stories bore little resemblance to their modern avatars. They were generally tales of heroism, about fierce warriors who slew animals and monsters who preyed upon humankind. The purpose of these stories was to stimulate a sense of shared values among members of a community. Campfire tales were told in this tradition for thousands of years. With the passage of centuries, they became the means by which elders passed on the wisdom of the race to the younger generation. Rituals built around bonfires and ceremonial fires invariably involved the telling of tales that explained beliefs that defined the tribe.

The origins of the contemporary campfire tale are found in the folklore and tall tales that evolved during the settling of America. These stories helped to populate the wilderness with recognizable human characters and give a tangible, if highly imaginative, shape, to things that lurked in the shadows just beyond the firelight. As handed down to Boy Scouts, Camp Fire Girls, backpackers, and the attendees of summer camp, these stories also foster a communal spirit, albeit with a somewhat different purpose from their primitive models: they keep the group together by scaring us with the frightening possibilities of what can happen to those who stray too far from the pack. Unravel any spooky campfire tale, supernatural or not, and you find threads of the same lessons running through them:

Don't wander from the path.

Don't go off by yourself.

Don't go poking into things unknown.

Don't do anything anyone else wouldn't do.

The most effective campfire tales are exercises in atmosphere, and the best told tales are models of performance art. They use the local color (almost always a rural or remote setting) and the time of day when they're told (the night) as a springboard for the scary. And they turn the noises of an evening in the woods into the soundtrack for the horror movie your mind makes of them:

That's not the wind you hear whistling in the trees: it's an earthbound spirit rustling in the undergrowth.

That baying of dogs coming from across the lake? You always hear that on a night when someone is going to die.

Of course not everything you hear but don't see in the woods is a supernatural monster. That twig you just heard snapping is probably the footstep of the deranged mountain man around these parts who keeps a collection of human heads in his cabin.

And what's making that low droning sound behind the insect chitters and frog croaks? Well—if you want to know *that* bad, you can douse the campfire and see what leaps on top of you!

Campfire Story

Legend: A ghost story told around the campfire proves to be narrated by a real ghost.

We were sitting around the campfire that evening trying to think of spooky stories to tell one another, since that was what you did on a campout. At first, no one wanted to say anything. A couple of us told stories that were more silly than scary.

Then, the person sitting directly across the fire from me spoke up. I couldn't see who it was, but he said he had a story that might chill us.

What did we have to lose?

You may not know it (said the storyteller) but this camp is pitched on ground overlying a natural cave system that honeycombs the mountain. There are miles and miles of caverns hollowing out the mountain. Much of it has never been seen by men.

Three years ago, I set out with Tom and Jack, my two best friends from college, to explore those caverns. There were rumors of treasure to be found in them.

A century before, a band of settlers known as the Daniels party had been set upon by Indians while traveling around the mountain range. They fled to the foothills and took refuge where they thought they could make a stand. To their surprise, they discovered that what they thought was a culvert actually was an opening to an underground chamber. Every member of their party carried as many of their valuables as possible into the cavern. Thinking to better their chances of survival, they split up into two groups and set off on two different paths of tunnels into the mountain. By prearrangement, they planned to leave the caves two days later. One group emerged as planned and found the horses taken and the supplies stolen by the Indians. They waited another full day, but the second group never came out. Several of the settlers managed to make it on foot to the nearest town, seventy miles away. They returned with military assistance and searched the caverns as best they could, but they never found the missing half of their party. It was assumed those men, women, and children had lost their way in the caverns. It horrified the others to think that even as they were giving up the search, those luckless people might still be trying desperately to find their way out.

This is what we had read in a diary of one of the survivors that Tom had stumbled across in the special collections library at school.

It didn't take much to persuade us that an exploratory trip would be the perfect cure for boredom that summer. Tom and Jack had caving experience, and I'd done some rock climbing. We figured that was all the training we would need as a team.

Tom had copied a map out of the settler's notebook. Incredibly, a century after it had been drawn, it led us right to the cave's opening. We had to clear scrub from the mouth and pry out a few large rocks that the rains of a century had brought down from the mountainside. When we worked the last one free, we smelled that musty minerally smell you find only in subterranean passages, and we realized we were inhaling air that hadn't been breathed in a hundred years.

It wasn't long before we found the chamber the settlers

had described—maybe a quarter-mile's trek inside. It was huge, with a vault so high you couldn't see the top even with the aid of the flashlights we carried. The ceiling and floor were punctuated with stalactites and stalagmites that made it look like we were walking into a monstrous tooth-filled mouth.

Just for the hell of it, Tom told us to shut off our lights. He wanted to show me how dark it got underground.

Have you ever seen total darkness? I mean a total absence of ambient light. There's nothing to compare it to. It's so black that you can put your hand an inch in front of your eyes and not even see it. I don't recommend it. You know in-stinctively when exposed to it that human beings aren't meant to live in such total blackness. It could drive a sane person mad in a very short time.

We hadn't carried much gear with us. We didn't think we'd be in there that long. We knew more about the caves than the settlers from the West had—not only how to get into them, but how to get out. Common sense told us to fol-low the tunnel with a draft blowing from it. To this day, I still think it was the best choice. But we had no idea what diffi-culties lay ahead. Parts of the path inclined so steeply that we had to rappel down them with ropes; parts were little more than ledges ringing bottomless pits. At one point, we had to worm several hundred feet through tunnels barely wide enough to accommodate the girth of our bodies.

We had been underground for maybe three hours when our flashlights picked up a scrap of cloth. It was blue ging-ham, and I could tell from the coarseness of the weave that it was very old homespun. We saw the bones shortly after. Not a complete skeleton. But enough for us to know that it was human. Shreds of the same blue cloth clung to it. Sinews still held part of the leg together, and we could see it was seriously fractured along the lower half.

Was this all that remained of the Daniels party?

It was Jack who noted the abraded, burnished surface of the bone. Something had been whittling away at it. Bats, we told ourselves. It had to be bats that had gnawed it. What else could it be? Right?

It was probably thinking about bats that set our imaginations running. Suddenly it seemed to us that the cave was alive with noises: chitterings, flappings, and scrapings against the stones around us. Sounds are funny underground. Drop a stone and you'll hear the noise of its impact echo off a wall, then another, then another. The ricochet seems to amplify the sound a thousandfold. And because you can't see walls, it's hard to pinpoint where the sound is coming from.

The noises we heard couldn't be explained as just dripping water, or wind soughing through the tunnels. Something was down there with us.

Jack and I agreed that it was time we headed back. Tom wasn't happy. He wanted to explore further. He knew better than to put up a fight, though. If Jack and I elected to go back, Tom would be on his own, and you never go that deep into a cave by yourself.

Still, Tom decided to show his anger at us. He was walking point, and every so often he would turn off his flashlight to tease us. He was carrying the power torch, and when he shut it off, the feeble glow of our flashlights only reminded us of the encroaching darkness.

The sounds seemed to be homing in on us, and Jack and I were getting spooked. When Tom turned off his flashlight for the third time, we both yelled at him. When he didn't put it back on, Jack went stumbling up ahead, ready to call Tom out. But Tom wasn't there. There were no side caves, and there was no way Tom could have advanced forward without a light to guide him. It was as though he'd been whisked away into thin air without our hearing or seeing it.

Jack and I panicked.

Our big mistake was to run back instead of running ahead. I don't think we were paying much attention to where we were going, because somehow we hit a stretch of loose rock we hadn't walked over before. We both went sprawling. I felt myself tumbling against jagged rocks that scraped and cut me as we plunged over the side of something. There was a drop of about ten feet that stunned me.

When I regained my senses, I looked for Jack. He was only a few feet away from me, but it took several minutes to find him. When you can't light up more than a circle a few feet around in the dark, you'd be surprised how much farther distances seem.

Jack had a serious head wound. He was still breathing, but I knew that without medical help he would soon be lost. We had fallen into a cavern that was impossible to escape from. Its ceiling was perhaps twenty feet high. There were one or two openings in it, but the walls were sheer and slick with mineral residue. There were no handgrips or toeholds. There was much on the floor to trip over in the darkness, but nothing big enough for me to pile up to reach the openings.

Jack died with his head cradled in my lap.

His flashlight had been lost in the rockslide. Mine was the only light source left. I tried to save the batteries by shutting it off for several stretches, but I couldn't stand the darkness. It only seemed to multiply the sounds of scraping and chittering that had followed me through the hole in the ceiling. When the batteries ran out, I closed my eyes and tried to pretend I was just going to sleep. The sense of suffocation, the overwhelming conviction that there were things waiting in the dark, just beyond my reach, to clutch at me, was maddening.

After two days, I was delirious with hunger. We hadn't packed more than quick energy snacks for the trip and I had exhausted those soon after landing in the cavern. I knew that I was doomed, but even a doomed man has a survival instinct that forces him to extremes of self-preservation. It helped that I never had to look at what I resorted to eating.

In a few days, even that supply had become inedible. But I was beyond caring. The sounds in the cavern had become deafening to my ears. Now and then I could have sworn I heard a faint human voice among them. But I never knew if it was real, or just my fancy tortured by fear and deprivation. The last thing that I recall was an absence of sensation, as though I were being absorbed by the very blackness around me.

The storyteller paused, and we all waited. After a minute Terry, who was sitting next to me, coughed impatiently. When we could take the silence no more I urged the speaker to finish the story, and tell us how he managed to escape the cavern. But there was no response. Later, we would all discover that each one of us sitting around the fire had thought it was the person directly opposite us who was telling the tale.

No one could explain how all seven of us had suffered the same hallucination.

Nor could any one of us explain what we found in the ashes of the burned-out fire next morning: the bones of a human hand, stripped down to the skeleton.

The last two joints of the little finger were missing, and appeared to have been nibbled off.

Initiation into Terror

Legend: A prank designed to make a house look haunted goes awry—and reveals that it actually is haunted.

The Crawford house had been abandoned for as long as anyone could remember. It was a decrepit Victorian mansion that sat in a weed-infested lot on the outskirts of town. No one ever claimed to have gone inside or even to have stepped on the property, although plenty of people dared one another to. There was something unhealthy about the atmosphere of the grounds. Something evil. It was said that if you stared at one of the broken attic windows long enough on a moonlit night, eventually you would see movement inside.

As president of his fraternity, Harry decided that the pledge initiation would take place at the Crawford house. It wasn't surprising that his frat brothers weren't too thrilled with the idea.

After fortifying themselves with appreciable quantities of alcohol, the boys set out for the dreaded place. There was much wild talk and roughhousing on the way there, but it all stopped once they stood outside the forbidding wrought-iron gates that enclosed the grounds. The house seemed to drain the courage out of everyone.

Harry found a break in the fence around the back. The two pledges squeezed through first, followed by their eight brothers-to-be. The first of the pledges shivered visibly in the misty night air, even though he wore a windbreaker. Harry laughed at the kid's show of nerves, but not too loudly. He felt the chill himself. It was as though the temperature had dropped five degrees once they passed through the fence.

They found the sidewalk up to the front of the house and navigated the broken flagstones and monster-sized clumps of crabgrass that turned it into an obstacle course. At the front porch they made a gruesome discovery: the carcass of a dog that had been dead for some time. In the light of their flashlights they could see the bones beneath the weather-tanned fur. There didn't seem to be much substance to the corpse. No one could figure out why the thing had strayed onto the property, or why it hadn't run away before it died.

Harry joked that it was actually a pledge who'd failed his initiation the year before. No one laughed.

The ritual was kept as simple as possible. The pledges were to go in one by one, carrying flashlights. There were three stories to the house. When each cleared a floor, he was to shine his flashlight through the front window of a landing. If he made it to the top without turning back, he passed the initiation.

Only the full fraternity members knew that Harry had arranged for Brent, a mountain-sized brother who played on the football team, to sneak into the house before sundown and hide in the attic. He was going to dress up in a black sheet and scare the bejeezus out of the pledges as each came up.

Harry motioned to the first of the two pledges to step forward. When the guy showed reluctance, Harry sneered that no one would really think the worse of him once word got around that he'd chickened out of his fraternity initiation.

Through the broken windows, they could all hear the pledge's footsteps on the first floor as he made it to the landing. When his light shone through the window, everyone gave a halfhearted cheer of encouragement. The clumping up to the next floor took just a bit longer. For a second time, the assembled boys in the front yard cheered the light shining through the window. The stairs on the third floor creaked miserably as the pledge ascended to the attic. It seemed to take him much longer getting there. Everyone waited anxiously below for the light in the window.

But all that followed was a scream of stark terror that abruptly cut off in mid-howl.

Harry and his brothers turned to the second pledge with looks of mock horror on their faces. They urged him to run into the house, telling him it was his responsibility to the fraternity to make sure that his brother was all right. They all knew that by now Brent had shucked his sheet long enough to show the first pledge who he was. Brent would instruct the first pledge to hide and then Brent would repeat his routine to frighten the second one.

They almost had to push the second pledge bodily up the steps. The kid was whimpering like a baby, and only the most dire taunts could get him moving. When the pledge's flashlight appeared at the first window, they all egged him on with catcalls and whistles. Someone started a countdown, and they all took up the chant as they heard him clump up the stairs to the second floor. The light shone through the second-floor window and the chant dwindled as they all waited for what they knew they would hear.

Creak! Creak! Creak! went the stairs up to the attic.

Once again, a shriek of absolute horror cut through the night. Something went flying out the attic window to land in the grass by their feet.

It was the second pledge's flashlight.

Everyone howled uproariously at how well the initiation had worked. Harry yelled up to Brent to bring their new fraternity brothers back down with him.

They all waited several minutes, but no one came through the front door. There was no tread of footsteps on the stairs, and no sound of any relieved conversation between the boys in the house as they reveled in their membership.

Suddenly, there was a scurry of movement through the overgrown grass behind them. Something large and lumbering and breathing heavily bore down upon them.

Brent!

He was struggling for breath, clutching the black sheet beneath his arm. And he was full of apologies for being kept so late at football practice that he couldn't make it to the grounds until now.

The fraternity brothers piled into the house, brandishing their flashlights. There were nine of them against whoever else might be inside, and they were all comforted by that fact.

None of them had been inside the house before, so none could have known that the stairway up to the attic was a narrow, rickety snake of steps that admitted only one person at a time. Moving cautiously in the lead, Harry slowly ascended and pushed around the bend the stairs led up.

The fraternity brothers waited breathlessly at the bottom—

—until Harry gave out a howl more ungodly than anything the pledges had unleashed!

The others all fled pell-mell from the house.

Dawn was breaking when the fraternity members who had participated in the initiation rite returned to the Crawford House. They were accompanied by the police, who were not amused at a fraternity prank and its apparently tragic consequences. It was the police who found Harry, huddled in a corner of the attic, sobbing prayers in a confusion of phrases that weren't meant to fit together. Harry's bloodshot eyes bugged in madness at some distant point no one else could see. His hair had turned completely white, and he never spoke another sensible word for the rest of his life. Two officers carried him down the steps, supporting him under the arms, and when he saw Brent's black sheet billowing in the hands of the cop standing by the cruiser, he screamed so horribly that he had to be sedated.

They never found the bodies of the two pledges.

Funhouse of Fear

Legend: The scary corpse in a carnival funhouse is a real corpse.

Kevin Clark was crazy about the carnival. It came to his town at the end of every summer and he could not recall a single autumn of his twelve years that he hadn't gone to see it. He knew every one of its rides and attractions by heart: the double Ferris wheel, the gypsy fortune-teller, the shooting gallery, even the freak show. But Kevin's favorite attraction was the funhouse.

He could always spot it from the midway: a squat, black building that looked like a clutter of giant shoe boxes of different sizes lying end to end. The weather-beaten black exterior was decorated with garish drawings of victims being chased into the mouth of a huge skull by a variety of monsters: cyclops, mummies, werewolves, giant two-headed human beings with three arms, and living corpses. The monsters were painted in slashes of bright red, green, and black that seemed to glow brighter than any of the midway lights. The people being chased always looked like they were screaming at the top of their lungs.

Kevin liked nothing more than to be one of those people.

He knew the layout of the funhouse by heart, and had for some time.

But this year, something new had been added.

The end of the funhouse walk was lit by a solitary overhead light bulb. Kevin had spied a flutter of movement near the bulb. He had nearly reached the hall's end when he heard a loud creak, and something bulky dropped down from the ceiling. The light flared bright with shocking intensity, and Kevin found himself standing face-to-face with a corpse dangling from the end of a noose. Hands slack at the sides suddenly reached up to grab him.

Awesome.

Kevin thought he might be able to convince some friends to come and see the thing, before he remembered that tonight was the last night of the carnival.

Then, he thought about how cool it would be to actually steal the corpse. He could just imagine the looks on his buddies' faces when they walked into his bedroom and saw the guy hanging there!

Kevin was scheming so hard that he didn't look where he was going on his way out and nearly tumbled over the little man who ran the funhouse. The guy was a short little lump of puffy flesh, with misshapen, muscular limbs and a hump on his shoulder that threw his whole posture out of alignment. The guy fixed him with an evil look. He was gargoyle-faced, with snaggled teeth, and a squashed nose beneath a mop of hacked, greasy blond hair.

Kevin knew most of the carnival barkers on sight, but he had never seen this guy before. He was as new as the corpse in the funhouse—and about as ugly! From the look the guy gave him, it seemed as though he knew that Kevin was thinking he belonged inside with the rest of the horrors. Kevin felt a tingle of fear until the lumpy little creep turned back to taking tickets from the next group of funhouse victims.

Kevin walked the fairgrounds for another hour, killing time. He made some halfhearted attempts to throw Ping

Pong balls into gold fishbowls, and pitch basketballs into hoops, but his thoughts were on the funhouse and how he might steal the dummy.

At one booth he was trying to concentrate on throwing darts at balloons pinned to a painted piece of plywood when he got the feeling he was being watched. He shrugged it off, but when he went to throw, his arm was jostled, and the dart flew shy of its mark. He turned around quickly, and could have sworn he saw a bush of unruly blond hair disappearing between people in the crowd behind him.

He got that tingle again, but shook it off. Probably just feeling nervous about what he was going to do.

At midnight, a voice came over the public speaker system telling the crowd that the carnival was closing down, and to please start heading home. Now was Kevin's chance. When he'd left the funhouse, he'd seen the back door: just a loosely hanging piece of black canvas. It would be a cinch to sneak inside during the confusion of everyone leaving the fairgrounds. He could have the dummy in his hands in a few minutes and take it out through the gates with him. Lots of other people were carrying stuffed animals, and no one would suspect that the dummy wasn't something he'd won at one of the games. The carnival guys probably wouldn't know that the dummy was missing until the next town they set up in—and then it would be too late for them to come back looking for it.

By the time Kevin reached the funhouse, the lights shining on the painted front were all off, and the gangplank leading up to it had chains across it. Kevin made sure no one was looking, then ducked under the wires put up to keep people from straying off the path in front. With the lights off, it was darker in back than he had thought it would be.

Suddenly, his leg snagged on something. It was a trap! He barely had enough time to move his arms in front of him before he went sprawling facedown into the grass and dirt. He shifted around, his heart pounding in his chest— and laughed nervously. He'd just tripped over a rope anchored to the ground by a stake.

The back door to the funhouse beckoned, and Kevin was surprised to discover that it was completely open. All he had to do was slip behind the flap and he was in. It was like they were begging someone to come in and rip them off.

It took a moment for his eyes to adjust to the dim light inside. He felt his way along the wall, but the weird angles made him uncertain of where he was.

He was feeling his way along the wall when something smacked him across the face. It was hairy and smelled disgusting as it pressed against his mouth. He spluttered and gagged against it.

With a laugh, he realized it was a fake arm that had shot out of the wall. He remembered how he had dodged it during his earlier walk through. Kevin felt a floorboard wobble beneath his shoe, and when he lifted his foot from it the arm pulled back. It was on some kind of spring that the funhouse visitor activated by stepping on the floor. That was probably the way all of the funhouse frights worked.

The dim yellow light was shining down on the hung corpse as Kevin groped his way to it. They hadn't even bothered to hoist it back up after the last show. Probably just left it there so that it would be easier for the short little creep to take apart when they packed up the carnival that evening.

He twisted the dummy around and saw it was locked into a harness with struts that extended into the arms. So that was how they made the hands seem like they were clutching at you as it bounced at the end of the rope. All Kevin had to do was lift the dummy up to free the harness from the hook that attached it to the rope.

Creaaaaaaaakkkkk!

A floorboard sounded behind Kevin. He instantly turned to stone.

Creaaaaaaaakkkkk!

There it was again.

He thought about bolting back the way he had come. But he'd already put so much effort into getting this far, it would be a shame not to follow through.

Creaaaaaaaakkkkk!

He was just being a kid. There were probably lots of loose floorboards in the rickety building that were making the noise. The funhouse had scary things in it—but nothing real.

Kevin turned around and embraced the hanging corpse, his hands clasping just behind the harness. The thing's bobbing head nodded down and its face rested against his cheek. He felt the icy coolness of a mask. It was solid black plastic, with a shiny surface that caught the light and reflected it in strange ways so that it would look like it was grinning or snarling, depending on your point of view.

Up close, he realized the dummy had a gamey smell—sort of like the dead animals he occasionally came across in the woods. He'd have to spray it with something if he was going to hide it from his mother inside the house.

The hook didn't give easily, and Kevin lost patience. He gave it a sharp tug. The dummy slipped out of his clumsy hands, and as he went to grab it he awkwardly pulled on one of the arms. He heard a papery crackle and felt it wrench free of its socket.

Damn! He broke it.

The detached arm slithered out of the sleeve, the hand still snug in Kevin's grasp. It had a knoblike bump protruding from its end, and Kevin held it up to the light.

Then he dropped it as though it were red hot.

It was a bone! A human bone!

The dummy spun around and Kevin gingerly reached up and flipped off the plastic mask.

The face behind it was mummified, the skin gray with the texture of leather. A filthy gag was tied around its mouth, but the dried-out skin had pulled in and Kevin could make out perfectly detailed skeletal teeth in the gaping mouth.

This was no dummy!

Kevin stepped back, gagging.

A pair of hands reached out from the wall behind him and grabbed him!

He stepped off the board, trying to make them retract and let go of him, but no matter how his feet danced over the surface the arms held tight. Then one of them grabbed him by the hair and roughly spun him around.

Staring back at Kevin was the leering gargoyle face of the ugly man!

The man smiled at him and laughed. Then he brought down something hard and painful on Kevin's skull.

When Kevin came to, he found that he could not move his limbs. They were bound to something hard and un-yielding. His chest felt constricted, as though there were cords wrapped around it, attaching to something behind him. And a nasty tasting piece of cloth stretched around his mouth, making it difficult for him to make any noise.

Kevin felt himself twirled around and came face-to-face with the funhouse dwarf. The man stared at him and stroked his face with the cracked fingernails on his filthy hand.

Such a good-looking boy. Much better looking than he was. But too nosy for his own good.

Kevin tried to scream but could muster no more than a gurgle against the wadded cloth in his mouth. He flailed his legs, only to find that he was no longer standing on the creaking boards of the funhouse floor. He was several feet above them.

The dwarf tugged Kevin's head roughly, forcing him to look down at the shriveled remains of the funhouse corpse, lying on the floor.

What a shame Kevin was such a mischievous boy. And how sad that he'd gone poking into things he shouldn't have, just like the last mischievous boy the dwarf had known. Now Kevin would have to replace what he had broken.

The dwarf snapped something over Kevin's face. Something dark and tight. Something cold and plastic that would hide his tears.

Why don't we give you a tryout right now? asked the dwarf, and Kevin felt the support he was standing on give way and he plummeted into space.

Kevin's disappearance was a complete mystery to his family and friends.

Eventually, they assumed he'd run away with the carnival.

Body Snatched

Legend: A physician is horrified to discover that a cadaver for his class is a person he recognizes.

Arthur Jepson, a leading London physician at the end of the nineteenth century, was spending his usual late hours in his surgery, conversing with his daughter Felicia, when a loud pounding sounded at the surgery's service entrance.

Thump! Thump! Thumpthumpthump!

Jepson recognized the loud knocks as the prearranged signal he had been anxiously awaiting. Pleading business that had to be attended to, he ushered his daughter to the front door and wished her well on her visit to an ailing aunt across town.

Jepson opened the back door to find Simon Fledge and Burke Townsend standing outside in the freezing rain. Unbeknownst to his colleagues, this unsavory pair were Jepson's stepping stone to his reputation as the physician with the best attended clinical surgeries at the university.

Jepson studied only the freshest corpses.

And Fledge and Townsend were his exclusive body snatchers.

The two men entered bearing a familiar canvas bundle, the wind howling as they wrestled their burden through the doorway. Each wore a sheen of ice on his grimy overcoat that attested to a lengthy interval outdoors in the miserable weather.

They slammed the shrouded body on the surgical slab and demanded their payment for services rendered. But Jepson insisted first on inspecting the cadaver. The class he would use it for was very important to his career. The retiring chief of hospital would be attending, and rumor had it that Jepson himself was on the short list from which his successor would be selected.

Several times in the past, Jepson's hirelings had brought him corpses still suspiciously warm to the touch. Such was not the case this evening. This cadaver was in a dismal state of disrepair. The flesh was mottled with splotches of decay, and the muscles of the face had pulled back the mouth in a hideous rictus. The chest was nearly caved in, shards of rib protruding through the graying flesh. Jepson remembered reading of an omnibus driver who had been run over by his own cab. It had happened a week before.

Fledge spoke up, pointing out how the cadaver's limbs were still supple like the doctor asked for. To illustrate, he flapped the arm hanging off the table like a limp rag doll. Jepson ran his fingers over the flesh and noticed that the anatomical landmarks of the elbow and wrist were all but absent. He felt bone fragments grate beneath the pressure of his finger.

The doctor whirled on his employees in a rage.

Did they think he was an idiot? He could tell when a joint stiffened by rigor mortis had been pulverized with a hammer! The corpse was putrefying. It would burst like an overripe grape if he attempted to stick a scalpel in it. He would not pay them a penny for this travesty!

Fledge was indignant. They had tried to find a fresher corpse, but there were none to be had. The authorities were closely watching the plots of recent burials and regularly monitoring undertakers who in the past had been easy to bribe. As it was, they had risked their necks digging for hours in frozen ground almost as solid as marble. They had performed their duty as best they could under the circumstances and demanded to be paid—or else.

But Jepson was implacable. If anyone would end up swinging from the end of a rope, he assured them it would be those two louts! It was crucial that he have a fresh corpse for the morning's lecture, and they were to procure one for him at any cost!

Mumbling imprecations, the two men slunk out through the door into the worsening storm. Jepson set about dismantling the useless corpse for burning in the oven, fulminating against the imbecility of his associates.

It was not until an hour before his morning surgery that the sleepless doctor heard the telltale knocking that signaled a new delivery. Fledge and Townsend bustled through the door with another shroud that hung limp between them like a sack of winter turnips. Though unwieldy, the bundle was not as heavy as the last, and they were able to heft it to the cleared surgical slab with a minimum of effort.

Jepson feverishly consulted his watch, knowing he had little time in which to groom himself before his lecture. He could tell by gore seeping through the top of the shroud that the cadaver was as fresh as any teaching physician could hope for.

Perhaps even fresher.

He was just preparing to unsheathe the upper body for inspection when the corpse shuddered beneath his fingers—

—and sat bolt upright on the table!

A shriek broke from its mouth—a horrible, demented wail that might have woken the entire neighborhood were it not muffled by layers of blood-clotted canvas.

Frantically, Jepson bellowed for Fledge and Townsend to

help him. But the two were cowering in horror against the door. Never in their lives had they witnessed such a spectacle! Jepson searched anxiously for a mallet, or any object heavy enough to smash the body into unconsciousness. Then his eyes picked out the syringes arrayed on a leather apron. He had been preparing specimens that evening and knew which of the needles contained strychnine. Even a small dose would shut down the breathing center of a living creature, forcing suffocation without any damage to the external tissues.

Moving quickly, Jepson extracted the syringe from the apron and jammed its point into the approximate abdomen of the corpse. He evacuated the syringe's contents with a deft depression of the plunger.

The corpse spasmed visibly, straining against cerements of canvas and hemp, and then pitched backward onto the table, landing with a flat *smack!* It continued to twitch periodically as the poison worked its horrible effects on the living tissues.

Fledge and Townsend had fled the surgery during the commotion. It was just as well, as Jepson's surgical assistants chose that moment to show up, signaling that it was fifteen minutes to lecture. They gaped in disbelief at the haggard man who stood where they had expected to see the usually dapper doctor. Mumbling excuses, Jepson performed his ablutions at the sink, telling the two men to prepare the corpse quickly for the surgical arena.

Jepson entered the surgery feeling the effects of the night's ordeal. But as he moved comfortably into his lecture the assurance that had won the confidence of others and helped him talk his way out of potentially criminal situations returned. He was succinct. Perspicacious. Brilliant.

The caul of sheets had been peeled back from the cadaver's head. The features were all but unrecognizable as human, so fearsome was the bludgeoning the head had sustained.

Jepson informed the class that they would begin with a dissection of the upper extremity to study the tortuous path of the brachial plexus as it innervated the muscles of the arm.

He freed the arm of the cadaver from its wrapping—

—and screamed hysterically.

Dangling from the corpse's wrist was an item his assistants, in their haste, had neglected to remove from the remains: a charm bracelet.

Jepson recognized it as the one he had given Felicia on her birthday not two weeks before!

Fledge and Townsend were never found. It was assumed the two had left town only half a pace before the law.

Jepson was convicted of murder, but his sentence was commuted to life imprisonment once it was understood that he had been driven quite insane.

Felicia Jepson's death was officially attributed to secondary strychnine poisoning which hastened the effects of severe head trauma.

Her death certificate was signed by an intern who had been the star pupil in Jepson's toxicology class.

The Summer of Cropsey

Legend: A woodsman named Cropsey, deranged over the loss of his family's land, preys upon the children who attend the camp set up on it, in the belief that blood sacrifices to ancient spirits of the land will rightfully restore it to him.

Camp Beechside was once the most highly regarded of all the summer camps that hug the foothills of New York's Catskill Mountains. But a visitor to it today will find its footpaths unkempt and overgrown, its cabins dangerously ramshackle, and its once pristine lakes stagnant and thick with algae. Camp Beechside has been closed to campers since the fateful summer of 1968.

The summer of Cropsey.

At the time no one really knew for sure that John Cropsey was more than the stuff of campfire stories. Not the townspeople, who saw their businesses wither and die with the bad publicity he brought. Not even the survivors of his onslaught against Camp Beechwood. The only people who were certain that Cropsey was more than just the figment of a vivid imagination were the ones who would never share their secret knowledge: his victims.

It hadn't always been that way. Once, John Cropsey had been known as one of the biggest landowners in the county. His family had handed down titles to hundreds of acres of forest and meadow over seven generations. The

Cropsey family had lived peacefully off their land all that time, keeping mostly to themselves and making only occasional trips into town to trade crops and furs for staples.

Their solitary frontier lifestyle was rudely interrupted by the postwar development boom. Businessmen from the city eager to take advantage of the burgeoning vacation trade began buying land out from under families whose roots had been sunk in it for centuries. What they couldn't buy, they took outright. John Cropsey was driven from his family land by politicians in the pocket of the resort financiers. He and Zachariah Cropsey, his teenage son and only blood kin, mounted a futile stand that ended in Zach's death from a shotgun blast fired by a state marshal. John Cropsey fought until his own rifle misfired, taking the last two fingers on his right hand in the explosion. Maimed, he fled into the wilderness of lands once his own, and eluded so many attempts to capture him that eventually he was given up for dead.

Wrongly.

The wilderness is no place for a man bearing the wounds John Cropsey suffered in body and soul. There's a darkness at its core that draws out the blackness of the ordinary heart. There's a quiet that forces a man's thoughts in upon themselves where they become ingrown and painful. There's an evil that flourishes like weeds along the byways of the wilderness and taints the vulnerable in spirit.

Some say John Cropsey went crazy in the woods.

It wasn't but a short time later that people in the area began to notice thefts. Workmen grooming the lands Cropsey once laid claim to, for a deluxe summer camp, reported the disappearance of tools carelessly left out at night. Farmers whose lands had been left untouched by the whirlwind of business speculators sometimes found their chicken coops broken into or their crops raided. Many attributed their losses to animals, or to mischievous children, who had begun attending the newly opened summer camps in droves.

One not so easily explained was the disappearance of a powwow book kept by the last descendant of one of the region's founding families. The book was a traditional compendium of folk wisdom, herbal medicine, and lore purportedly shared with settlers by elders of the Indian tribes who had once inhabited the land. Some say a powwow book is nothing more than a collection of wilderness tips tricked out as tall tales. Others hold that it is a powerful book of magic spells.

Its owner returned to his cabin and found it missing one day—that, and an old axe.

Who knows why Cropsey stole the powwow book or what he made of its content? There was much speculation, later, that his rage-disordered mind had interpreted a ceremony for the renewal of crops as a formula for restoring not only the lands taken from him, but also his dead son. How else to explain the rampage that occurred the first summer when weather conditions permitted the sighting of three successive full moons—the only circumstances under which a blood seeding could take place?

The first murder at Camp Beechwood occurred in June 1968, at the end of a drought-stricken month that weathermen were predicting was a harbinger of the dry summer to come. Jack Mann, a city kid in the last week of his month's stay at Camp Beechwood, had snuck away from his cabin that evening and struck out for the woods. On a nature hike earlier that day, Jack's cabin mates had told him about a special type of night-blooming flower that could be seen only by the light of the moon. They claimed to know a museum that would pay hundreds of dollars to anyone who could supply them with a specimen.

Jack didn't know why his friends laughed so much when they told him this. They said the flower shined with a special light that made it easy to spot in the dark, but finding it proved to be very hard work. And deadly as well, as Jack discovered later that night.

It was easier to hush up tragedies in the mountains back in 1968, and the local coroner was paid handsomely by the owners of Camp Beechwood to keep observations on the postmortem for little Jack Mann to himself. So very few people ever heard about the discovery of the boy's headless body—or the traces of iron that indicated he had been assaulted with a rusty axe.

Summer festivities at Camp Beechwood continued into July of 1968 as they had for many summers previous. The drought of that summer continued as well, and the parched conditions of the land were blamed for the next death that occurred on the camp's grounds.

With so little rain that month, streambeds had dried up into rock-stitched scars, and ponds had shrunk to mosquito-infested swamps. Only the main lake was big enough to sustain a program of water sports and play. Camp counselors had been enjoined to be extra watchful of the campers under them in the wake of the previous month's misfortune, and many of the boys chafed at the stricter rules and limits imposed on them.

In the last week of July 1968, Ken Kline secretly led his bunkmate and three other boys to the lake for a moonlight swim. Skinny dipping was forbidden under camp regulations, but Ken had managed at least one night of it without getting caught each of the past two summers at Camp Beechwood. He felt he was especially entitled this year because of the restricted lake time he and his buddies had been allowed during daylight hours.

It was a cloudless night and the full moon gave the lake's surface the look of a silvery sheet of ice. No persuasion was necessary to get the boys to plunge in and head for the center of the lake, where their shouts and yells were less likely to be heard. Though there were five of them, Ken could have sworn he heard a sixth splash after the last of them had cannonballed in off the dock. But the sound had seemed to come from the far side of the lake, and he decided it was just an echo of the last plunge.

The boys frolicked their way out to the middle of the lake, the slowest of them complaining that his feet seemed to keep getting tangled in weeds or something that none of the other boys had felt. It was he who proposed that they have a contest to see who could hold his breath underwater the longest. On the count of three all five boys gulped in air and dunked themselves.

The boy keeping count was the first up out of the water. He was followed in less than twenty seconds by the next two, gasping and laughing. The fourth boy emerged fifteen seconds later, spluttering that someone had tried to hold him under, although the others all protested that it wasn't them.

The four waited for Ken to surface. And waited. And waited.

After two minutes, they began to worry. It was typical of Ken to play the prankster. But *if* something had gone wrong, they would never be able to find him in the murky nighttime waters.

They had just formed a wide circle and begun calling his name when Ken surfaced. His body shot up as though it had been hurled from the depths, then smacked back down with a loud splat. The boys realized something was wrong when Ken failed to respond to their praise for how long he had stayed under. Swimming toward him, they saw him lazily bobbing facedown in the water.

A turbulence in the lake heaved an unexpected wave up and the terrified boys saw the cause of Ken's listless floating.

There was nothing left of him from the shoulders up.

Ken Kline's fate was officially attributed to "death by misadventure." Shortly afterward, stories of Cropsey began making the rounds of the weekly campfires at Camp Beechwood. None of the campers who heard them dared to stray from the marked paths, or go wandering from the camp at night, after hearing how Cropsey was lying in wait.

It was during the final campfire of the summer season in 1968 that the last of the Camp Beechwood murders occurred. While the head counselor narrated the creepy legend of Cropsey to the wide-eyed campers sitting around the fire, members of the counseling staff snuck secretly into the woods, where they were to provide scary noises that would add to the nighttime atmosphere. But one of the counselors, Steve Bennett, had other things on his mind that evening. He knew there would be a brilliant full moon that late August evening, and he had made plans with Marilyn, a counselor at the girls camp across the lake, to rendezvous at a nearby ranger's hut. He knew the other counselors would be occupied with scaring the campers so he wouldn't be missed.

Steve found the door to the hut unlocked when he reached it. It was pitch dark inside but he could just make out the light color of Marilyn's blouse as he latched the door behind him. Before he could say a word, he heard a scurrying sound outside the window and a loud thump against the wall.

Steve froze in place.

A walk of crude wood planks circled the perimeter of the hut, and he made out the slow tread of heavy boots moving around it.

Shushing Marilyn so that she wouldn't make a noise, Steve crouched low to the floor and tried to match the footsteps outside tread for tread. He made it to Marilyn's side of the hut and managed to grab her hand, squeezing it in silent assurance.

The latch jiggled sharply.

Once!

Twice!

Steve held his breath as he heard something large and metallic clank on the rock doorstep.

As he waited for the prowler to go away, Steve decided it wasn't smart to stay in the hut. He and Marilyn could easily find a more romantic spot for their last night together. When the coast seemed clear, he took her hand and tiptoed stealthily to the door. Looking back over his shoulder as he unlatched the door, he was puzzled to see Marilyn's blouse still visible against the far wall.

Then the door swung open to let the moonlight in—and Steve saw that the hand he held was no longer Marilyn's to control. Pathologists would determine later that she had tried to protect herself, and that it had been lopped off by the same savage blow that had removed her head.

Camp Beechwood closed permanently the following day. The owners abandoned it shortly after, and when the wilds reclaimed it, the locals quipped it was as though the land had been returned to John Cropsey. Certainly, some of them believe in the stories of Cropsey, if only because of the evidence reported in affidavits filed at the end of the summer of 1968:

Outside the ranger's hut, a rusty axe with a weathered handle that bore print traces from a man lacking the last two fingers of his right hand.

And footprints in the dust surrounding the hut:

One set of prints leading up to it, but two sets—one made by a younger man—leading back into the woods.

Tales for
After Dinner

There's a mouse carcass at the bottom of the bottle of soda!

A favorite children's candy is made from spider eggs!

The meat in a popular fast food is made entirely from genetically engineered materials!

No story causes terror and revulsion like a good bad-food story. And why not? There is no relationship more intimate than that between the eater and the meal, and few betrayals more shocking than the discovery that one's food is not what one thinks it is.

Tales of bad eats are a staple of urban legendry. Most serve as an index to our suspicions that sanitation, hygiene, and quality control are not the foremost concerns of businesses where they should be of paramount importance. The greater our suspicion, the grosser the story. Surely everyone has heard the famous fried rat story: a man buys lunch at a franchise that specializes in fried chicken and is halfway through what he thinks is an unusually tough piece of breast meat when he discovers it has a tail (or whiskers or claws). Variations on this story sometimes involve hamburgers: the luckless customer takes a chomp out of his burger, only to see a tail sticking out of the opposite side of the bun.

One of the most gruesome food fiasco stories reflects distrust of food packagers who tout secret ingredients or all natural products. A woman with a violent allergy to mayonnaise buys a hamburger at a fast-food chain and tells the counter person she doesn't want any of the secret sauce the chain is known for because it contains mostly mayonnaise. She's eating the hamburger in the car on the way home and feels an ooze that tells her she's got a mouthful of mayo. She rushes to the hospital emergency room to head off the severe allergy attack she knows will come, and is informed that she actually bit into a cow tumor that was in the beef used for the burger.

The more ingenious food fairy tales have the makings of a good crime story. Consider the one about an outbreak of a mysterious illness never before seen in the United States. It's traced back to a food processing plant that enslaves illegal immigrants from a country where the disease is epidemic. Another has an intriguing plot worthy of an Alfred Hitchcock wrong-man mystery. A man eating in a restaurant bites down on something gristly and, not wanting to offend his dinner companions, spits it into his handkerchief, which he deposits in his jacket pocket. The meal over, the incident is forgotten. Weeks later, the police come to his door accompanied by the dry cleaner he left the jacket with. They show him that the handkerchief tucked into his pocket contains part of a finger (sometimes with a ring on it). The finger turns out to belong to a missing mob kingpin (or, in less remarkable variations, to a cook whose knife slipped while he was preparing the food).

The darkest of gruesome gobble legends evoke the horror of cannibalism. As films like *The Texas Chainsaw Massacre* remind us, the eating of human flesh is still regarded as one of the most unspeakable of all taboos.

Tales abound of people who accidentally or deliberately partake of their parents, sample their siblings, or feast on their friends. The shocks they give us are proof that even though you are what you eat, you can't eat what you are!

The Doom of
the House of Gaskell

The house of Gaskell was cursed. Since the turn of the eighteenth century, when it began to prosper wildly from the processing of sugar and rum on its island plantations, it had suffered the tragic deaths of all its firstborn male heirs.

Laban Gaskell was the first in the family's legacy of doom. A student who had interrupted his study of medicine to tend to family business, Laban had established the first of the Gaskell plantations. Within a year, he had contracted a terrible tropical illness that caused his skin to erupt in boils and fester on his living body. Before his brother Calvin could travel to his aid, Laban was dead and buried.

Calvin assumed his role as new head of the family and within two years of his arrival his wife gave birth to a son, Oliver. Oliver learned the family trade at his father's knee and proved to have a head for business. But within a week of the transfer of the family title upon his father's death, Oliver took sick with a strange malady that turned his flesh into a nightmarish corruption and swiftly claimed his life.

Oliver was succeeded by his younger brother Joseph, who recognized the similarities in the deaths of his brother and uncle Laban. From spies in the town, he discovered that a native family bore a grudge against the house of Gaskell for the usurping of tribal lands. It was rumored that the head of this tribal family, a drunken layabout, had put a dire curse on the Gaskells. Joseph was an enlightened man, but he knew an example had to be set. The native was convicted of witchcraft by the colonial court and led to the stake shouting oaths against the Gaskell name.

Joseph's son Colin was a rationalist like his father. He knew that his family's constitution was not suited to the tropical climate and reasoned that this was the underlying physical cause for the Gaskell curse. He urged his father to repatriate the family to their home in Scotland, and this Joseph did, leaving the plantations in the hands of the capable island managers. Colin helped orchestrate the return of his family and their possessions to their homeland. He had just begun to enjoy his position as the first absentee landlord in the Gaskell succession when he was struck down by the all-too-familiar affliction. The cooler northern Europe climate helped slow down the rotting of his animate body, but he died as miserably as his forebears and was buried in a shroud of crusted bandages.

And so it continued generation after generation. Each of the firstborn Gaskell heirs ascended to the lofty height of family patriarch. Each was felled in short time by the inescapable curse. Numerous remedies were attempted—even returning lands to descendants of the islander burned for witchcraft—but none helped. Each generation a new Gaskell heir sought to beat the curse. And invariably, within weeks of his majority being recognized, a younger brother was summoned hastily and secretly to assume the duties of his dying sibling.

Rumors abounded that the Gaskell heirs were victims of God's implacable wrath toward the prideful. The name of

Gaskell was recited from pulpits throughout the country as an example of the consequences that befell those who lacked true Christian humility. The family's history was mentioned in the Gothic romances and penny dreadfuls. The name of each new heir was whispered to small children to scare them into behaving.

Charles Gaskell was the last of the House of Gaskell, the only issue of his father Burton. The enormous burden of responsibility to his family, coupled with the probability of his imminent doom, had given him a dour disposition since childhood. As Burton lay in state in his chambers in the family castle, Charles accepted the mantle of his family in the timeworn ritual, just as every firstborn male child of the Gaskell line had. The family solicitor was called in, the necessary legal papers were signed, and Charles toasted his future with a glass of rum drawn from the family's private reserve. It was a gesture that symbolized the family's dedication to its business. This gesture, and death, were the only certainties the Gaskell heirs had known for nearly two hundred years.

Charles polished off the draught of rum, and was admiring the cut crystal glass that was now his own when he saw the dregs: bits of undissolved matter that coated the bottom of the glass.

Poison! he thought.

Immediately, the butler who served the drink was summoned. He in turn called for the steward. The steward protested his innocence, claiming that he had drawn the drink from the cask in the castle cellar that was reserved exclusively for the ritual of family succession. With the castle guard forming a cordon around them, Charles, the solicitor, the butler, and the steward marched down to the cellar.

Charles inspected the cask, a genuine antique that purportedly held what was left of the first rum distilled under the Gaskell name. It had been brought back to the family castle when the Gaskells had returned from the islands. Its staves were an inch thick, and so tightly grouted with tar and resin it was doubtful anyone could have introduced a poison into it. Nevertheless, it seemed more than coincidental that ten generations of Gaskell heirs had imbibed from it since Laban's time, and ten generations had died hideously.

Charles tapped the top near the spigot and the echo that resounded told him the cask was down to its lees. Without further ado, Charles instructed the sergeant of the guard to break the cask open.

What they found that evening finally explained the curse of the House of Gaskell, though it brought little consolation to Charles, who drowned in a pool of his putrefying tissues before the month's end. It took a doctor at the local hospital who was familiar with the family's tragic history to make sense of the evidence.

Calvin Gaskell was to blame, of course, for disposing of all of Laban's papers not related to the Gaskell family business, whether from ignorance or out of respect for his brother's privacy. There, most certainly, an account would have been found of Laban's efforts to study and understand the infection that took his life. It was incredibly potent, and frustrated his every effort to make sense of it. Laban knew he was dying, but he believed medical science would eventually triumph over such odious diseases given the time to study them and the physical evidence of their ravages.

Laban had made the ultimate contribution to the medical discipline he had turned his back on, with the help of servants who had followed his last wishes to the letter. More's the pity his family never consulted them.

They might have found out sooner that a cask of alcohol makes a perfect specimen jar.

Legend: When a family opens a vat of spirits they have drunk from for years, they discover that it was being used to pickle a corpse.

Secret Ingredient

Legend: A man eating at a restaurant discovers that the meat in his meal is not what it seems.

Jerry O'Neill tucked into his bowl of stew like a man who hadn't eaten in six days. In fact, it had only been six hours, but driving around in the backwoods in the rain, looking for the interstate and getting hopelessly lost, had somehow stoked his appetite.

He had found the dingy little diner entirely by accident. It was off on an unpaved road, barely more than a muddy trail, and it looked so decrepit he at first thought it had been abandoned. In a way, it was. When he stepped inside, he saw that he was the only customer. The interior smelled of stale cooking grease, and the menu felt like it. But it had a standard bill of fare, and Jerry wasn't inclined to be too picky.

The stew had a rich, savory broth, with succulent bits of meat swimming in it. It seemed almost too good for the surroundings.

He was glad he had taken his waitress's recommendation. Her heavy accent had prevented him from understanding anything else she said.

"What's good?" he had asked.

"Stew's good," she had said.

"What's in it?" he had asked.

"Stew's good," she had said.

Well, okay, the stew *was* good, and Jerry spent most of his meal silently trying to match the ingredients to the accent of the waitresses. Eastern Europe? Mediterranean?

He was almost done with the stew, and nowhere nearer an answer, when he crunched down on something hard. He tried to spit it out discreetly, but it had forced itself partly between his molars and he had to work a finger in to extricate it.

It was a bone—but not a bone like any he had seen before. It had a triangular shape, sort of like . . . what did they call those little bones in the spine? Vertebrae?

Jerry had never seen one this small before.

He was puzzling over his discovery when he happened to look down at his spoon. Sticking to the congealed goo on its edge was a hair. Too long to be one of his own. Too short to be from the waitress. Definitely from some kind of animal.

As though perfectly timed, he heard a loud snarl from the kitchen that ended with a definitive-sounding *THUNK!*

Jerry recognized the yowl of an angry cat—and the sound of a meat cleaver cutting it off.

He spit out the bit of food left in his mouth and pushed back from the counter, retching. This had to be some sick practical joke. Cat stew? You only heard about something like this in urban legends!

He was repulsed. But more than anything else he was angry! Sure, there were countries where house pets did double-duty as dinner. But this was America! You didn't serve people tabby treats in the USA!

Jerry bellowed for the waitress, and when she didn't come out from the kitchen he bellowed for her again.

Still no response.

He knew he should just get up and leave without paying. But he couldn't resist giving these primitives a piece of his mind.

Walking back behind the counter, he peered through the round window in the swinging kitchen doors, determined to get someone's attention. The windows were steamed on the inside, and he couldn't see a thing.

Pushing gently, Jerry opened the doors just wide enough to slip through. The kitchen looked like prep areas he remembered from his teenage years working at fast-food joints: stainless steel tables, utility sinks for washing dishes, a deep fryer, and a stainless steel range with multiple burners.

The place was as deserted as the front rooms.

An open pot hissing on the stove billowed steam around the kitchen. Jerry looked into it cautiously and could make out lumps of something blanched bobbing in a boiling froth. The smell coming from the pot was acrid, and Jerry felt his stomach lurch instinctively.

He called out a "Hey!" but there was still no answer.

A doorway in the back revealed a narrow hall leading to a dimly lit room. On his way to it, Jerry passed a butcher's block. A cleaver and a set of filleting knives were lying on its blade-scored surface. He had no doubt that this was where they clocked the kitty. But where was the bloody mess?

There didn't appear to be anyone in the back room, either. The bulk of the space was taken up by a walk-in refrigerator, and Jerry saw that the door was slightly ajar. If the waitress had stepped inside to retrieve something, she wouldn't have heard him yelling.

He pulled the door back.

There wasn't much to look at inside. A few cuts of meat, including a rack of short ribs, hung along the side. Jerry looked closer and got that clutching feeling in his stomach again.

He was looking at a human rib cage! It had been expertly dressed out and cleaned. A few ribs on the lower left side had been taken out by a sharp edge.

Arms dangled from meat hooks. Jerry counted three of them. The bicep of one had been expertly flensed. He didn't even want to guess what the loop of sausage casings hanging next to it contained.

This wasn't a refrigerator—it was a slaughterhouse!

Gagging, he backed through the door—

—and felt something sharp enter his back, just above the kidneys. Before he could even react, it had angled upward and jiggled swiftly to the left and the right. Something seemed to open inside him.

With a gasp he pulled forward, turning on his heel, clutching the side of the refrigerator door as his legs gave out beneath him.

He just had time to see a large man in a bloodstained cook's apron brandishing the wicked boning knife he had backed into. The man had a cruel smile on his face. Rubbing his head against the man's leg was a large orange cat. It still had all of its limbs. And Jerry could have sworn it licked its lips at him.

The first word that came to his mind was "Bait."

Several people were standing behind the cook: the waitress and others in kitchen garb. They all had the same crazed look in their eyes.

Hunger.

When Jerry had walked into this little greasy spoon, he had wondered, as he always did about places that had no business, how they managed to stay alive.

He knew now.

It wasn't by eating cat stew.

Just Desserts

Stella was looking forward to Christmas! She had spent much of the week decorating the house, wrapping presents, and organizing the family's traditional Christmas Eve dinner. This year, the menu was easy to plan. Her brother, Tadeuscz, had been sending home delicacies from America almost since his arrival four months before. He would be staying there for the holidays with Babcia, their grandmother, and Stella had decided that, to commemorate her absent brother, she would incorporate as many as possible of the foods he had sent into the meal at the family get-together.

Just two mornings before, the last package from Tadeuscz had been delivered by the postman. As usual, it came without an accompanying note—Tadeuscz preferred to send his letters under separate cover to save money—but Stella didn't need a note to explain the delightful candies, the delicious looking nuts, or the aromatic coffee.

To her puzzlement, Tadeuscz had also enclosed a tin of flour—hardly a gourmet specialty, even for Poland! What's more, Stella did not think it the best flour she had ever worked with. It seemed both coarse and flaky at the same time, and it had a sullied, dirty color, far from the bleached whiteness she was used to. Stella had sneezed all the while she sifted it for the Christmas dessert, and thought the stöllen she made from it flatter and denser than she ever remembered it coming out. She hoped that the fact she had used Babcia's recipe would compensate for its less than ideal outcome.

The dinner was indeed a success. Uncles, cousins, and spouses had toasted her grandly for the game birds filled with American chestnut stuffing, the sausages seasoned with American herbs, and the side dishes made from American wild rice. But no one toasted the dessert made from brother Tadeuscz's flour. When the stöllen was sliced and parceled out, she couldn't help but notice a quieting of her family's joviality. Faces turned dour, and the room grew ponderous and thoughtful, as she watched everyone work too vigorously to chew forkfuls of the sweet pastry, studded with candied fruits and nuts. Stella saw dishes pushed back not even half-finished, and the children—incredibly!—did not beg a second slice.

She considered her own reaction no less responsible for the dampened enthusiasm of her family. Midway through coffee and cake, she excused herself to the kitchen when she crunched down on a bit of food so unchewable its noise had raised the eyebrows of those around her. She had assumed it was a bit of almond shell—but in the kitchen, she discovered it was a tiny fragment of bone. She stared at the trimmings from the meats she had served and wondered how in the name of heaven she had been so careless in her preparations to allow what seemed to be remnants of the main course to taint the dessert!

On her way back to the dining room, she was bluntly admonished by her brother Jerzy, who always drank more than he should, that the stöllen was not anything like what Babcia used to make.

The coffee Tadeuscz had sent did much to improve the end of the evening, washing away the bad taste left by the stöllen. To sustain the celebration after the unwrapping of gifts, Stella opened Tadeuscz's Christmas card, which had arrived only that morning, two days after the package, to share the salutations in his enclosed letter. How could she have known the horrible pall his words would cast on the evening's festivities:

My Stella, our Babcia has died this week of an unexpected illness. I enclose in a flour tin of aluminum, which should not trigger airport metal detectors, the ashes of her cremated remains. Please spread them over our family garden in Lödz as she wished.

Legend: *A foreign family used to eating food sent them by a relative in America consumes the contents of one package—and later is told it contained the ashes of one of their relatives.*

Urban
Legends

Question: What's not quite a campfire tale, but something more than a simple superstition?

Answer: An urban legend.

Urban legends are modern tall tales. They take an aspect of modern life—the home, the workplace, a basic human relationship—and transport it into the realm of the comic or bizarre. Like any kind of legend, most urban legends torture credibility. But they play upon fears or anxieties that resonate so strongly with the listener they can't easily be dismissed. They can never be tracked to a verifiable source—but they're "known" to have happened to a friend, or friend of a friend. They are easily adapted to settings and situations familiar, and believable, to their credulous audience.

Their name notwithstanding, not all urban legends are concerned with the city. The term "urban legend" is used to distinguish a type of contemporary folklore different from the traditional homespun tall tales of earlier times.

A typical example of an urban legend is a story that began circulating this past decade, after it became common practice for firefighters battling raging forest fires to use helicopters that douse wide swaths of woodland with chemicals or water. Investigators going through one badly damaged stretch of forest after a blaze was extinguished stumbled upon the burned remains of a man dressed in a full wet suit and with a charred oxygen tank strapped to his back. After a week of head scratching, the investigators ran across a story in the news of a scuba diver who had been reported missing. Putting two and two together, they determined that when one of the helicopters that had been jettisoning seawater over the forest fire went to refill its tanks, it sucked up the luckless scuba diver and evacuated him with the water—straight into the heart of the inferno.

Another popular urban legend dates back to the 1960s, when contact lenses came into vogue as a popular alternative to eyeglasses. One day, an electrical worker was doing maintenance on some wires at a substation whose current had been shut off. A worker at a remote part of the substation, not realizing that power had been cut for a reason, threw the switch, sending a current into the line that badly shocked the maintenance worker. Although the man professed to feel all right, he was sent home for the rest of the day. As he prepared to lie down on his bed and sleep off the day's ordeal, he went to remove his contact lenses—and discovered that the current had welded them to his corneas!

Central to both these stories is the underlying concern of every urban legend: what happens when an ordinary situation goes alarmingly haywire and spins out of the individual's control. Common denominators of each—the luckless victim and the careless perpetrator—are found in virtually every one of the hundreds of thousands of urban legends in circulation today. Whether they expose the "real" ingredients in the food we eat, describe incredible mishaps on the job, summarize the misunderstandings between the sexes, or call attention to the mischief that children, animals, suspicious lovers, or teenage drivers can cause, urban legends are mirrors that reflect our willingness to believe that life is unpredictable and the world potentially dangerous. They're also pretty good barometers of the average person's gullibility.

Most urban legends describe funny or quirky situations that call attention to ordinary human fallibility. But some grow from the same raw fears that fuel horror fiction. A popular but unfounded legend about drug pushers who give kids blotter paper with cartoon character faces soaked in LSD captures our concern about the vulnerability of the innocent. Our fear of random acts of senseless violence is summarized in the story about gang members who drive without their car lights on and open fire on the first car to flash headlights at them. General squeamishness about bugs and nonhuman species are the foundation of the legend in which a girl dies from the bite of black widow spiders who have been nesting in her unwashed bouffant hairdo. And if you're the type of person who prefers the comforts of home to travel, you probably don't want to know all the stories about the couple who notice a strange smell in their hotel room and discover an aged corpse under their bed.

Most urban legends don't hold up under close scrutiny. But the more effective ones can raise a shiver of apprehension in the short time it takes you to ask "What if?..."

Brainy Type

Legend: Every school kid knows at least one teacher who sold her brain to doctors so they could study it after she died and find out why she was so smart.

E lsa Kincaid awoke with a start to a clinking sound.
Metal?

Glass?

She couldn't be sure. Her senses were fuzzy. Her ears felt as though they were plugged with cotton, and when she opened her eyes everything looked like as though it were covered with a film of gauze.

Where was she?

She struggled to remember, then checked herself. Hadn't she always told her students that you couldn't force your brain to answer a question? Patient study of a problem was how you arrived at a solution.

The haze before her eyes began to clear and she winced at the bright light shining into them. It was from a huge overhead bulb with a reflecting plate behind it. She could just make out the ceiling and the tops of walls, painted an off-white color that seemed to intensify the glare.

A harsh chemical aroma awakened her sense of smell. She inhaled through her nose and recognized the pungent, sterile odor of rubbing alcohol. It filled the air and seared the dried-out membranes of her nose as she sniffed.

Now she remembered: she was in her doctor's office. Dr. Stewart. Arthur Stewart. Little Art Stewart, who had been one of her best pupils in high school.

Elsa tried to turn her head, first left, then right. Something braced against the sides prevented her from moving.

She could tell she was lying on a firm padded surface. A flex of her arthritic fingers confirmed that it was a leather-covered examination table. Her right arm felt like lead as she tried to lift it, and it was some seconds before she realized she was trying to tug it up against resistance. Her left arm, too.

She was strapped down to the table.

What had happened? She knew that sometimes doctors restrained patients who experienced convulsions—but that wouldn't have been necessary for her. She hadn't been sick in years. Not even a cold! She had just come in to get her annual checkup out of the way before the holidays.

Behind her, she heard water running, and more clinking. Instruments of some kind, she guessed. They were being laid on a tray.

She tried to speak, but her tongue was a clod of dried clay in her mouth. Sometimes, when she fell asleep on her back, she awoke with her mouth so dried out she could only manage a feeble croak before downing a glass of water. This was worse. Her mouth felt paralyzed. Possibly . . . anesthetized?

What was going on? Had she experienced some kind of fit while Dr. Stewart was examining her?

Her mind racing, Elsa tried to reconstruct events as best she could remember. She had shown up for her 3:00 appointment exactly at 2:45. She had always stressed punctuality to her students, and lived by the same standards she held others to. She remembered thinking it strange that Arthur's receptionist was not at the desk when she arrived. Arthur himself had let her in.

There were no other patients in the waiting room. She assumed that she was the last of the day. No doubt, Arthur had started to cut back his workload. He was not well. She had heard rumors around town of his illness: brain tumor. How tragic, especially for so young a man.

In fact, Arthur had not looked well when he admitted her. He was gaunt and haggard. His thoughts seemed to wander when she made small talk with him. He avoided looking directly at her—the same way she remembered him doing when she caught him in a lie as a student.

He seemed distracted, too, and behaved in other unusual ways. He barely seemed to be listening to her as she chatted during the examination. His movements were lethargic and mechanical—the effects of illness, she assumed. His clinical detachment had made her feel uneasy.

It was Arthur who brought up the subject of their deal. She had laughed upon remembering it. Years before, when he had persuaded her to register for the organ donation program at the hospital he was attached to, he had quipped how he always wanted to study her brain to see what made her so smart. Laughing, she had promised him that when she was dead she couldn't think of anyone she'd rather let handle her brain than her prize student.

That was the last that she remembered of her office visit today—well, that and the shot Arthur had given her just after. Now, what had he said he was giving her the shot for?

He hadn't said—had he?

She could try to ask him now. He was hovering above her, his face darkened in the shadow thrown by the light behind him. The sickness made his eyes look strange. Elsa had learned to read faces well from all her years of teaching, and she saw desperation in Arthur's. Desperation was a powerful feeling, she knew. It could unhinge a vulnerable mind.

Elsa tried to talk but she couldn't make her lips form words. Then Arthur began talking, softly—and Elsa knew the hell of having to scream but not being able to make a sound.

He was dying—he knew she could see that. But he was determined to follow through on their bargain. A promise is a promise—isn't that what she once taught him?

Elsa heard the click of gears engaging, then a loud buzz. Arthur's face was replaced by the whirring blade of a surgical saw that slowly began to lower toward her face.

There was nothing to worry about—he would follow their agreement to the letter.

He promised she would be dead by the time he reached her brain.

Cocoon

Legend: *Earwigs have been known to crawl into the ears of sleeping humans. Because they can't turn around inside the ear, they tunnel through the brain to the other side. If the female of the species lays eggs inside the brain, her offspring will do the same when they hatch.*

Y ou are a doctor.
Your knowledge of medicine is second to none.

You know the name of every bone in the body. You can diagnose precisely without consulting reference books.

Your attention to clinical detail extends to your personal life.

You know exactly how long you have been having an affair with your best friend's wife: one year, ten months, thirteen days.

You know exactly how long you have wished him dead: one year, ten months, *twelve* days.

You have a foolproof plan.

It came to you one evening while you were enjoying your hobby.

You collect insects. You kill them and mount them. You derive great satisfaction from this pastime. You hope someday to discover a new species and have it named for you.

You are drawn especially to exotic winged creatures. Butterflies, moths, and . . . other things. You know of one species unlike any other. You are aware that in its larval stage it is a parasite with disgusting capabilities. It has been known to seek out the warmth of the ear's recesses. In blind insect fashion it gropes ever deeper, tunneling through the brain, seeking exit through the opposite ear. It feeds on the brain's soft tissues and fluids. The female of the species lays its eggs in the wall of the tunnel she creates. And when the hatchlings emerge, they mimic the parent: tunneling, feeding, reproducing. There is no cure for this parasite—only death of the host.

You know all this from descriptions of animal autopsies in the clinical journals you subscribe to. You don't know anything about this insect's effect on a human being, because the few known victims were mercifully killed and their bodies destroyed before the worst damage from the infestation occurred.

You suspect it must be a horrible way to die.

You know where this insect lives.

You know your best friend is traveling there.

And you have worked out a scheme to dispose of him. You will offer to give him the physical he needs to travel overseas. You will expose him to the larva when he is not expecting it. By the time you diagnose his symptoms upon his return, it will be much too late.

You know that acquiring this creature as a living specimen violates all customs and importation laws.

But you have friends in high places.

Your plan proceeds smoothly. Your friend appreciates you taking certain shortcuts to expedite approval of his and his wife's vaccination schedule.

You assure him, after the examination, that he is medically sound and will return the same way.

You wish him bon voyage. You kiss his wife good-bye and, with a wink, admonish her to take good care of him.

You wait and count the days, ever so patiently.

You check up on him upon his return a month later. You assure him that he looks perfectly fine. You listen to his complaints of dizziness and blame them on jet lag. You tell him they will go away with time.

You see him three weeks later. You express concern that he is having severe headaches. You ask him if he was exposed to any unusual allergens on his trip. You give him pills that ease his pain and mask the ravages of what is going on inside his head.

You rush to the emergency room three days later and express alarm that he is bleeding from his eyes and ears. You say that even someone with your well-known expertise encounters medical enigmas that he cannot explain.

You take a complete medical history, and you shake your head in puzzlement—frequently.

You run a routine series of X-rays and concur with the technician that there is no visible evidence of anything amiss. You administer stronger medications that have little effect on your friend's constant suffering.

You wring your hands conspicuously.

You finally order sophisticated diagnostic studies. You ask the radiologist if he has ever seen anything resembling the faint, swollen track through the brain his computer-enhanced images have picked up.

You help restrain your friend when he begins convulsing.

You step back in well-rehearsed alarm the day the insect emerges from the other ear. You crush it beneath your feet as it tries to escape and enjoy the charade of crude medical triumph.

You soothe your friend's teary wife before your astounded medical colleagues with the assurance that the worst is now past.

You study your medical books when his condition does not improve.

A week later you tell him about the eggs the insect laid in its tunnel. You make sure he understands the implication of what you are saying. You prescribe a sedative when he begins to scream.

You eat a sumptuous meal that evening.

You check in on your friend periodically and try to comfort him.

On the day he lapses into a coma, you tell his wife to make preparations.

You are present in his room the day he dies. You were right about it being a terrible way to die.

You are the attending physician, so you sign his death certificate. You smile inwardly as you attribute his death to "parasite infestation of foreign origin."

You resist the temptation to order an autopsy. You are curious to know what your friend's affliction looks like clinically. You are, after all, a doctor. You would like to examine him directly, to see the corruption he has become a vessel for. You know it might generate a publishable article. But you are also a very cautious man. You want to ensure that nothing can be traced to you.

You help the family make your friend's funeral preparations.

You spend the evening enraptured with his wife.

You attend the wake the next day. You have recommended a closed casket.

You deliver the eulogy at the prayer service. You sing the praises of your friend. You shed tears of admiration for his dear wife's fortitude.

You support her on your arm as the two of you approach the casket. You kneel and pray with all the fervor you can pretend.

You pause momentarily as the mourners throng about the room. You could swear you heard a sound issuing from the casket. You steal a glance at your friend's unreacting wife.

You startle when you hear the sound again. You think it sounds like something scratching from within.

You wonder if it isn't just your guilty conscience.

You genuflect and rise, reminding yourself how unlikely this explanation is.

You stand in consultation at the back of the room with your friend's wife and the priest. You exchange banalities about what a good and decent man he was.

You hear a stirring from the front of the funeral parlor. You stop what you are doing when the thumping begins. You crane your neck above the whispering mourners to see the commotion up front.

You glimpse the coffin bouncing on its gurney. You watch it rise and fall again, and then again. You wonder what the hell is going on.

You hear the sound of splintering wood. You see the mourners stumbling over one another, fleeing. You hear their screams as something thrusts itself through the coffin lid.

You can't believe your eyes.

You think you see the reticulated joints of an insect's leg. You know there is no insect leg the size of a man's. You watch another leg force a hole through the coffin lid. You stand mortified as they plant themselves against the wood and flex upward.

You see the lid explode up off the coffin. You feel detached from your body, as in a dream.

You see something huge and ghastly crawl from the interior. You note how it shucks off the skin of your friend's desiccated corpse. You think it looks like nothing so much as a butterfly emerging from a cocoon.

You know that this is no butterfly.

You see it flap its wings, then jump toward you. You note its stinger dripping venom on the carpet. You hear two sets of mandibles clack asynchronously. You see four multi-jointed legs clutch in your direction. You sense a wind from rapidly beating wings. You see your face reflected in two huge obsidian eyes. You know the eyes reflect sheer malevolence.

You marvel at the new species you have brought into being—the one that by rights should bear your name.

But as the creature swoops down upon you, you realize there are some abominations so horrible that they cannot be named.

Mule

Legend: Drug dealers sew shipments of drugs into the corpses of babies who are carried through customs by smugglers posing as parents.

Mike Long was a kidnapper who worked the south Texas territory. His routine was very simple: He snatched babies from families vacationing in the Texas border towns and smuggled them over to Mexico. From there, the kids entered the vast underground network of the baby black market. Where they went or what use they were put to after Mike turned them in was no concern of his. He was strictly in business for the money.

Mike was skulking outside the customs booths when he pegged a young American couple for his latest hit. They had just crossed over from the Mexican side, probably on their way back from a day trip. The woman was carrying a blanketed bundle over her shoulder, and Mike figured it for a kid no more than a few months old.

Mike liked infants, but not for the reasons most people did. They were easy to run with. They didn't put up much of a fight. And as merchandise, they had fewer identifying marks. His bosses would be happy. And happy bosses meant a pocketful of pesos.

Mike fell in behind the couple, sizing up the guy. He

looked wiry, but not the type who'd be much of a problem to handle. The woman didn't strike him as the mother type. She looked more trim and fit than he would have expected for someone who'd dropped a stork's egg only a short time before. But Mike had no reason to believe she wouldn't respond the same way they all did. Get the drop on daddy, and mommy gets so flustered she doesn't even think to hold junior too tight.

They had reached a part of the parking garage that Mike had scoped out for some time. It extended down and around the corner and was full of dark shadows. No one indoors would hear any commotion.

Quickly, Mike moved forward, a sap in his right hand. He went to strike, but the guy turned around unusually fast, almost like he'd been waiting for someone to come at him from behind. The lead weight caught him on the side of his neck, but he grabbed Mike's arm and took him down in a tumble.

Mike had his gun out. He'd never fired it before because he hadn't needed to. One wave of a pistol and the smart victims backed off, usually with their hands up. This guy wasn't too smart. He was wrestling Mike for the gun, as though his life depended on it. In the scuffle, it got jammed up under the guy's chin. When the idiot tried to pull it out of Mike's hand, the safety popped and Mike felt the trigger squeeze under the pressure of his finger.

Bam!

The guy's throat muffled the report of the gun. It also spattered Mike gruesomely with blood.

Mike was up in a second, heading for the woman. Incredibly, she didn't scream for her husband. She was looking for some way to escape without having to go around Mike. When Mike reached for the baby, she didn't offer any resistance. Instead she just backed up against the wall of the parking garage until she was flat against it. Her eyes never left him.

What an ice queen.

Mike thought about popping her for good measure, but decided every second spent on this side of the border was a new nail in his coffin. He was out the ground-floor door and on the street in a second.

With the baby tucked securely in the crook of his arm, Mike moved from shadow to shadow thrown by the buildings. It was imperative that he avoid being seen—at all costs. A man with a baby would surprise no one. A man covered with blood was a memorable sight, even in parts of the country where life was cheap.

Mike was craning his head around the corner of a building to see if the coast was clear when he felt his bundle slip. Instinctively, he fumbled for the child, who was pretty light for his size. The child made no sound and Mike thanked himself the kid was a sound sleeper. He hoped junior would stay down for the count for the next hour.

Moving through alleys, Mike snaked his way to the outskirts of the town. The police would probably have been alerted to the death of the American by now, and it was just a matter of time before they closed off the border. He'd timed his hit so it would be dark enough to slip over the border, but not too dark to see on the other side. Moving agilely, he sprinted from behind the garbage shed of a border cantina. The river was narrow at this point. Fording it would throw police dogs off his scent.

The baby bobbed on his shoulder, oblivious to his exertions, and to the blood and sweat that had begun to stain the blanket.

Once on the other side, Mike doubled back to a shantytown that he knew to be in this part of the desert. Coyotes ferried wetbacks from here. Drug dealers dispatched their mules from here. And baby smugglers picked up their cargo here.

He had just reached the shantytown, when he tripped on a rock in the darkness. He couldn't control his balance, and went face forward into the dirt, his tiny burden beneath him. Briefly, he felt something jam against his rib cage before it gave way sickeningly and flattened beneath him.

Sitting up, he plucked the silent child from the ground and gingerly peeled back the flap of blanket from his face.

The kid was dead. There was no doubt about it. He'd seen enough dead kids in his line of work to know.

All that work, and he'd ended up cashing his meal ticket!

Then Mike noticed a gash in the skin on the kid's head. Blood should have been gushing from it, but nothing was coming out. In fact, there was no rosy pink look to the skin like he knew other babies had. Mike poked his fingers into the swaddling to probe for a pulse in the kid's neck.

There was none. The kid's skin was ice cold.

A feeling of nausea billowed in his stomach. Mike had carried back over the border a baby that had been a corpse before the first crossing. He looked back toward the direction from which he'd come.

What kind of twisted perverts were those two people?

Mike didn't want to know. He sought the nearest pile of trash in a back alley and carved a kid-sized hole in it before planting the baby.

When he turned around, there were several flashlights shining directly in his eyes. Instinctively, he put a hand up to shield them, forgetting to draw the gun from his belt. That's what the light shiners were waiting for. One clubbed him with a sawed-off baseball bat, and Mike went down hard.

He awoke to find himself securely duct-taped to a chair

in a dark room. A single desk lamp was lit on a table next to him, and Mike knew what the blanket-wrapped bundle on it was. Squinting against the light, he made out men on the far side of the room hammering something together.

Off to the side the ice queen stood talking to a large man. When he saw Mike stir, he stepped forward and spoke to him in a soft, accented monotone. Mike had caused him no end of trouble. Thanks to his intervention, a shipment was late and schedules were behind.

The man plucked the child's corpse from the table, and Mike stared at it in puzzlement. The kid's belly was crudely stitched along a cut that ran from neck to groin. The guy flicked a switchblade out and deftly sliced the stitches. When he reached into the incision Mike turned his head in disgust.

The man slammed something down on the table to catch Mike's attention. It was brick-shaped and wrapped in plastic. Mike knew immediately what it was. Its street value would have made it unnecessary for him ever to work again.

Mike knew the ruthlessness of the drug cartels. For the first time that day, he was scared for his life.

Mike had killed one of the best mules in the business, he was told. He would have to pay them back by taking a double shipment across the border.

Mike nodded his agreement. He'd carried drugs before. A guy like him might look funny carrying a pair of swaddled babies over the border, but he'd do anything to get out of there.

The men on the far side of the room stopped hammering and moved toward him. Behind them he saw a rough wood box that he thought looked a like a full-sized coffin.

Then the men took out their knives.

And Mike knew how they were going to package the double shipment.

Coat Carrier

Legend: A woman buys a fur coat and is bitten by a snake nesting in its lining.

For the fourth time that day, Susan Jay felt the hem of her overcoat snag on her stockings. Craning her head over her shoulder, she saw the telltale run down the back of her leg that told her she'd just lost another pair of stockings.

Damn!

She'd had nothing but bad luck with her clothes since she'd bought that coat. She was beginning to wonder if it was cursed.

It had been a last-minute purchase. Not that she hadn't been looking for nearly two hours in the department store for a warm winter overcoat to go with her dark outfits. But it wasn't until the closing gong sounded that she spied the coat hanging by itself on a rack outside the changing rooms. It was plush and furry, and just the right size for her slim build. The coat was a mottled, natural color that wasn't quite what she had envisioned, but she wondered if maybe that opinion was influenced by the fact that the manufacturer wasn't one of the better-known designers.

Susan inspected the label to see what the coat was made of, but there was nothing that gave her a clue. She flagged down a tired-looking sales clerk, who perked up notice-ably when she realized that Susan was a potential sale. The woman launched into some double-speak about a type of fur from some rare animal in some unpronounceable third-world country Susan had never heard of. She sur-mised that the clerk had a prepared sales patter to cover up the fact that she knew nothing of what she was talking about.

The closing gong sounded a second time, hastening Susan's decision to buy the coat. She didn't want to take a chance on wearing some endangered species that would get paint-bombed by the anti-fur fanatics—but neither did she want to risk leaving the coat for someone else to buy and having nothing to show for her two hours of work.

While the clerk checked her credit card status, Susan tried the coat on one more time.

Looking in the three-way mirror, she thought it seemed to hang a little lower to her right—which was odd consid-ering that when she had held it up on the hanger, it seemed to hang a little bit lower to the left. When she couldn't find anything stuck in one of the pockets that might be weighing the coat on one side, she chalked it all up to some hidden anti-theft device, or maybe the mirror's reversal of images.

That evening, when she got back to her apartment, she performed her usual ritual of greeting her parakeets, which were among the few animals on her landlord's approved pet list. The birds went ballistic, thrashing against the bars and putting up a ruckus that would have scared off any cat within three blocks. Susan couldn't figure out what was wrong with them until she pulled her coat out of the shopping bag and the birds became even more frenzied. She wondered if the fur the coat was made from was from some kind of natural predator of parakeets. The birds would probably be fine once the coat had had a good dry cleaning. And her dry cleaner could no doubt tell her just what kind of fur the coat was made from.

Yesterday, on her way into work, she'd found a tear in her blouse that she knew had not been there when she'd dressed that morning. She suspected a stapled tag or hidden straight pin lost in the coat's lining, but when she inspected it at her office she could find nothing the fabric would have caught on. On her lunch hour, she felt an unusual chill on the back of one leg and discovered a jagged tear in her leggings, just below the level of her skirt. Something sharp in the lining of the coat had to be moving around and causing all this damage to her wardrobe, but she was damned if she could find it.

Susan's grouchy disposition over the loss of today's nylons wasn't helped any by the bus home, which was crowded and overheated. She was hanging by a strap, pressed between businessmen with briefcases, when she felt a wiggle across the back of her thigh. She turned to glare at the jerk behind her—and then felt something slither across her stomach.

She screamed as something stung her sharply just above her navel. Then stung again. And again.

People squirmed away, trying to give her space as she frantically thrust her hands inside the coat. Her fingers came out with smears of blood on the tips.

Clawing at the inside of her coat, Susan loosened a seam in the lining.

A thin black snake, over a foot long, slid out over her arm and plopped to the floor.

Susan fainted.

She awakened to the sound of a telemetry monitor and the smell of disinfectant that told her she was in the hospital emergency room. A young doctor was swabbing her abdomen with a cool cloth, and Susan was propped in such a way that she could see a series of pinpoint tracks along the skin, right where she had felt the sting.

The doctor was very kind with his explanations, assuring her that the snake that had bit her was not poisonous, and that the bites would do well treated topically. The snake had probably crawled into the coat where the importers had shipped it from. Probably smelled the fur and recognized it as an animal common to wherever it lived. They'd inspected the coat thoroughly and could assure her there were no more lurking reptiles.

Susan felt squeamish about wearing the coat home, but it was cold outside and she had little alternative. Snake-free or not, she was taking it back to the store the next day and demanding a refund.

She was just crawling into bed that evening when she felt an itch along her side. She idly scratched it, but that only seemed to make it worse. She wondered if it was the effects of whatever the emergency room physician had coated her with.

Suddenly, her skin felt like it was on fire.

She ripped back the covers and pulled up her pajama top. An army of mite-sized bugs was swarming over her abdomen. Some had burrowed in, and Susan could see a florid pattern of hemorrhages coalescing under her skin.

Horrorstruck, she saw a black swath of the bugs cutting across the carpet from the end of her bed to the door. They seemed to be pouring out of the coat. Before the pain became too excruciating, she made it to the phone and managed to dial 911.

The only one who could explain the weird bug infestation was the pathologist who performed the post-mortem on Susan's ravaged body in the morgue. He knew of these insects. They burrowed in the hides of one particular species of animal native to his country and laid their eggs in it. When the young hatched, they fed on the animal's blood. For that reason, import of the fur outside the country was strictly forbidden.

Usually, the pests were not a problem. There was one natural predator whose diet consisted mostly of these insects. It sought them out and was responsible for destroying most of the population.

It was a special kind of thin black snake. . . .

The Giving Kind

Legend: A man awakens from a drunken one-night stand and discovers that one of his kidneys is missing.

Paul Marks awoke to the sensation of fire and ice. The fire was an excruciating burning pain in his low back. The ice was what the bathtub he was sitting in was full of.

Groggily, he shook his head, trying to clear his thoughts as much as his vision. The movement sent up his back searing pain that made him wince.

What the hell had happened last night? He remembered cruising the bar scene, and catching the eye of one beauty who, incredibly, was all by herself at the watering hole. He sent her a drink that led to her beckoning him over, another drink, small talk, more drinks, and finally a trip back to his place. Paul tried to recall what had happened the rest of the evening, but a dense bank of fog had settled over his brain, and he realized it was going to take some time to dissipate.

He had awakened with intense hangovers before, but this was the first time he'd wound up in an ice bath. What kind of preferences did this indicate for the lady? Or, for that matter, for himself?

The cold was starting to numb parts of his body that shouldn't be numbed. He placed a hand on either side of the tub, but the strain from trying to lift his body out aggravated the intense pain. The last time he remembered feeling such agony was prior to his appendectomy three years before. He fell back onto the ice, which only made him fccl worsc.

Had he gotten so acrobatic the night before that he'd slipped a disc? How else to describe this debilitating pain?

He couldn't remember the woman's name, but on the off chance she was still in the apartment he called out a generic term of endearment and asked her to help him. After a half minute of no response, Paul realized he was all alone.

It was then that he noticed a distinct reddish tinge to the water in the ice bath. It reminded him of the bottom half of a tequila sunrise. He saw that it was getting redder by the second.

Slowly, so as not to irritate his painful back, he snaked his hand through the icebergs in the tub to feel along his spine. Just above his pelvis, he felt some rough foreign object. His fingers were getting more numb by the second, but he worked them along the tender area of his low back. Whatever it was that wasn't his skin, it extended along several inches. And there was a warmth oozing from it.

Ohmigod! I'm bleeding!

With a strength that came from adrenaline more than muscle, Paul managed to heft himself over the lip of the tub. He hit the floor knees-first and felt his funnybones send flares of discomfort along his legs. He crawled and slid through the puddle of ice water on the floor, over to the sink, and used it as a support to pull himself up.

His back was pulsating and every throb felt like a sledge-hammer whack.

Hunched over, with his fingertips pressed white against the blue ceramic of the sink, he turned his aching side to the mirror. Just to the left of his spine, he saw a lattice of cross-hatched filaments that he recognized as a crude approximation of surgical stitching. Blood was seeping at an alarming rate from an incision that had been imperfectly closed up.

Somehow, Paul managed to find a bathrobe and stumble out to his front room—which was a scarlet nightmare. There were splashes of blood—his blood, he assumed—everywhere, save for a perfect square in the center of his once white carpet. Someone had probably laid a tarp down before cutting into him.

But why?

His legs gave out just as he made it to the easy chair. Groping for the phone, he saw a scrawl on the top page of his memo pad, made with lipstick. Through his blurring vision, he read:

Sit as still as you can and call 911 immediately.

Paul did just that and was connected to a dispatcher. His vision was slowly fading from color to a photo-negative tint. He was barely able to choke out his name, address, and problem. The dispatcher told him he recognized Paul's situation, and to sit tight. They would be there right away.

Assured of rescue, Paul promptly blacked out.

He awoke to that same fuzzy feeling he had endured earlier that day. This time, thankfully, there was no pain. He was numb from the neck down and lying on his stomach on a gurney in his front room. Through hazy vision, he saw men dressed in white hospital scrubs milling around him. A confusion of medical terms was being recited over him.

He tried to lift his head up, but the muscles in his neck were slack. Clearly, someone had seen his effort, because a voice that he recognized as the dispatcher's began talking soothingly to him.

They had reached him in time. He was the latest victim of renegade organ harvesters who supplied healthy specimens for the black market. Their methods tended to differ, but frequently they used a woman to lure a man home from a bar, drugged his drink with a potent anesthetic, and then performed surgery on the spot. Sometimes, they didn't bother with the niceties of wound closure and stitching. He was very lucky to be alive. The woman last night had removed one of his kidneys. It was a good thing she had left the other one.

A very good thing.

Paul was too anesthetized to digest the full horror of what the EMT was telling him. He sensed the man moving behind him.

He wouldn't believe how much people in desperate need of a transplant would pay for a kidney, a lung, even a heart, the EMT remarked from behind him. It was a very lucrative market.

Paul heard a noise that sounded like a sharp edge slicing through paper. Dimly, he saw a stream of something shoot over his shoulder, and realized, without feeling, that it was his own blood.

Not only was it lucrative, the EMT continued.

It was also very competitive.

Crazy Sally

Legend: The shy, unassuming woman next door is secretly a murderer.

Crazy Sally was crazy about her lover's face. She knew all its lines and creases, its many soft curves and sharp angles. Sometimes, in the morning, she would lie awake for hours, gazing raptly at its features, memorizing its contours with the tips of her fingers.

The brow was an impressive brow, high and prominent. Sally had always thought that a strong brow was the sign of a strong mind. Sometimes Sally wondered what thoughts went on behind that brow, and whether she could ever understand them all. Her own brow was not so big, and so, she guessed, neither were her thoughts. But she had thoughts that were not so easily understood either. She knew she did! She had surprised her lover with them once, and that was proof.

His eyes were quite remarkable. The sockets deep set but level to give them a penetrating gaze. Behind the shut lids were the brightest blue eyes she had ever seen. "Baby blue," she called them, but there was nothing young about them. The almost imperceptible wrinkles at the corners were a clue to their age. These were eyes with experience. They had seen quite a lot—not all of it pleasant. Sometimes Sally thought those eyes could look right into her soul. Yet there was still innocence in their look, for Sally knew they could not see everything.

Her lover's nose was a marble sculpture, a Grecian ideal of beauty made flesh. It helped to accentuate the sharp cheekbones, and divided the face with geometric precision into absolutely perfect halves. There are two equal sides to everything, Sally would say. Just look at my lover's face.

The lips were perhaps the most remarkable feature of her lover's face. Thin, but not so thin that they did not feel full and inviting when crushed against her own. More than the brow, more than the eyes, more than the nose, it was the lips that best captured the expressions of Sally's lover. Relaxed, they were a study of contentment. Turned down, they were a road map of dissatisfaction. Sally preferred to think of them turned up, in happiness and laughter. It was these lips, so firm but gentle in their line that shaped the words her lover spoke to Sally. Those words often amazed her. They spoke of important things she sometimes did not understand. They spoke tenderly of Sally and the affection her lover felt toward her. Once they had spoken harshly. Once they had called Sally crazy.

Only once.

But Sally realized that that one cruel insult helped her to remember her lover's kinder words all the more sweetly.

Sally would spend the rest of the morning looking at his face and thinking thoughts of love, until the alarm clock rang, reminding her that she had to go to work.

Reluctantly, she would put her lover's face back in the refrigerator where she had taken it from.

The rest of the day would be an empty and unfulfilling until the evening, when Crazy Sally could return home to contemplate her lover's face again.

Slumber Party Terrors

The scariest urban legends and campfire tales are based on fears that show us all to be children at heart. Small wonder, then, that so many feature children. You can't ask for a better representative of human vulnerability than a defenseless child. Nor can you ask for a more sympathetic victim than a child at the mercy of irresponsible adults.

Kids are subject to all manner of dismal fates in urban legends. They are strapped into car seats accidentally left on top of cars that drive away. They're forgotten inside vehicles left in sweltering parking lots by harried, forgetful parents. One of the more bizarre legends of inept parents has a frantic mother rushing her sick infant to the hospital and accidentally backing her car over an older child trying to help out.

Leave a child in the company of a negligent or incapacitated caretaker and you're just asking for a sad outcome. For example, there's the well-known tale of the intellectually challenged babysitter who has a surefire method of keeping her infants docile: when the child cries, she just lays him in the oven and soothes him with the lulling hiss of the gas. Senile grandparents charged with watching infant grandchildren have been known to confuse directions from their kids to put the baby to bed and the roast in the oven.

Occasionally, tales of this type take a turn into the Grand Guignol. Perhaps you've heard the one about the husband and wife who were leaving their child in the care of a nanny while they went on a two-week vacation. The nanny was running late and phoned to tell the parents just to leave the child buckled into his high chair if they were afraid they might miss their flight. The parents did so and left. The nanny was struck by a car en route to their house and killed. Two weeks later, when the parents returned . . .

Unlike the many real-life horror stories we read in papers, urban legends about children unsupervised by adults are less concerned with the mischief the kids get into than with the horrors waiting to take advantage of them. An entire subgenre (which has been rigorously mined for Hollywood teen flicks) involves babysitters, slumber parties, and even innocents fresh from home, at college or in their first apartment, being preyed upon by those criminals with a nose for the naive. These stories depict the hitherto secure home as a useless refuge against those with evil on their mind, and suggest that for every independent kid, there's at least one burglar, psychopath, or knife-wielding maniac who knows they're home alone.

Don't Turn on the Light!

For the past week, the newspapers had been full of warnings about the Campus Creeper. A student had been killed coming home on her own from a fraternity party at 2 A.M. the Friday before. The police thought the murder might have been committed by someone she met at the party, but they had no leads. In the days that followed, several coeds had reported they thought they were being stalked.

That cold November night, on her way to the campus library, a junior named Mary Crane realized she had forgotten her psychology notebook and would have to go back to her apartment to get it. The path back wound through several poorly lit blocks. She found herself walking quickly between streetlights. She had heard that muggers weren't likely to attack you if you walked with authority, and she guessed a brisk stride of fear wouldn't look any different from a brisk stride of confidence.

Halfway home she was certain she heard footsteps behind her.

Tap, tap, tap, tap.

A steady staccato that perfectly echoed her own.

She slowed her pace.

Tap . . . tap . . . tap . . . tap.

The echo slowed accordingly.

Mary felt every muscle in her stomach clench. She

rounded a corner and pressed herself into a shadow made by the wall.

The echo stopped.

Turning her head for a better angle to see, she brushed against a stalactite of icicle that hung from the ledge just above her. Dislodged, it fell to the ground and made a noise of impact:

Crack crack.

Mary started, then studied the shards of glistening ice at her feet. She tapped her foot once on the sidewalk.

Tap tap.

She did it again.

Tap tap.

She tapped both feet one after the other:

Tap tap. Tap tap.

She stifled a nervous laugh with her mittened hand. She'd been running from the echo of her hard-soled boots off the walls of the huddling apartment buildings!

When Mary got home, she opened the door to a pitch-black apartment. She could hear her roommate Chris's harsh, slow breathing in the corner where the couch was. Mary waited inside the door for several seconds, hoping her eyes would accommodate, but it was no use. She really didn't want to put the light on. It would only disturb her roommate and make her cranky. Besides, she really didn't need the light. She knew exactly where her notebook was.

Four steps from the doorway, her foot connected with a soft lump on the floor. She nearly went sprawling over whatever Chris the slob had dropped there.

From across the room, Mary heard a rustling noise. Maybe Chris was dead to the world, but her roommate's dog, Ralph, was alert. At least as alert as a dog awakened from its slumber would be.

Mary advanced cautiously across the room, her left

hand out, and her right hand down at her side. She felt Ralph nuzzle her mitten tentatively.

Three more steps and her outstretched hand brushed the wall. She gently moved her right hand until it connected softly with a table against the wall. She was moving her hand over it, feeling for the telltale coil of metal on her notebook, when Ralph's persistent head brushed her leg.

"Not now, Ralphie, not now," she hissed.

Not to be put off, Ralph pressed the bulk of his body against her leg.

"I said not now!" She shoved Ralph with her leg, her frustration putting more heft behind it than she'd intended. Her hand lighted on the notebook as the dog skittered back against the table. Something—a video?—clunked loudly to the floor.

Mary stood stock still, hoping that Chris wouldn't waken. She was rewarded by the steady saw of breath over on the couch.

Could sleep through an earthquake, she thought.

When Mary heard Ralph's paws scrabbling clumsily for purchase, she knew what that meant: he thought it was play time. *Oh no.*

She spun on her heel and headed for the door, remembering to sidestep the bag on the floor. Her bearings were perfect, and she was back out the door and locking it behind her as Ralph's body *galumphed* against it on the other side.

Back walking on the street, Mary was tucking the notebook into the stash of papers and books in her backpack when she heard the echoing footsteps again. She smiled, and stopped.

She'd heard a footstep that wasn't an echo.

She summoned all the authority that she could—and sprinted for the library.

*   *   *

Mary returned to the apartment at eleven that evening. The study session at the library had gone well, but she had been annoyed to discover that Ralph had ruined her jeans. Someone in the study group had pointed out the stains on her pants, and asked what she had brushed against. Looking at the long dark streaks down her legs, Mary knew. Nosy Ralph had gotten into a mess.

When she got home and found the apartment door unlocked, it didn't even occur to her that something might be wrong. Chris sometimes ran laundry down to the basement without taking her keys. But the light was still off, and Mary slapped at the wall from the doorway until she found the switch.

What she saw forced a scream from her like none she had ever made before. Inside the doorway, Ralph lay in a pool of blood, his legs splayed at awkward angles and his eyes glazed in death. Chris lay by the couch, a crimson nightmare.

From the apartment of a neighbor awakened by her howl, Mary phoned the police. Their investigation did not take long.

Mary revisited the evening's events for them: how she had returned to the apartment around seven and found nothing amiss, how Chris had been sleeping fitfully on the couch, how Ralph had pestered her all the while.

The police exchanged glances with one another, then broke the news. The medical examiner placed the time of death an hour *earlier,* not later. The dog had been killed before that. It had taken Chris a while to die.

Mary looked at them in confusion. That simply wasn't possible. Ralph had been alive and frisky. She had the stains on her pants to prove it.

The medical examiner inspected the stains. They were blood, he told Mary. But the streaks were too widely placed to be from dog claws.

They had saved the worst horror for last. Leading Mary back into the apartment, they guided her around the tarp that covered Ralph's body, to the bathroom. There she saw the mirror, and the message that had been daubed on it in her roommate's blood:

Aren't you glad you didn't turn on the light?

Legend: A college student returns to her dorm one evening to pick up books she forgot. Not wanting to disturb her roommate, she doesn't turn on the light. When she comes home from studying, she finds her roommate dead, and a message from the killer scrawled in the roommate's blood on the bathroom mirror: "Aren't you glad you didn't turn on the light?"

Final Call

Legend: A babysitter pestered by phone calls that threaten her and the children with bodily harm calls the phone company to complain she's being harassed. The phone company traces the calls and gives the babysitter the horrifying news of where they are coming from.

Sixteen-year-old Lucy Clark was babysitting the Dillon kids the night of the breakout at the state hospital. The first phone call came at 8:20, minutes after the radio station had interrupted its regular programming to report the killer's escape.

Lucy wondered if it might not be Mr. and Mrs. Dillon, calling to tell her they were coming right home. Not likely, she realized. The play they were attending would already be into the first act, and the odds were no one had a radio on at the theater.

She picked up the receiver, scrabbling through the papers on top of the table for a notepad and pen with her free hand.

A monster's roar blasted out of the earpiece:

"I'm coming to get you, Lucy!" it growled. Then, immediately, the voice changed to a high-pitched laugh that she recognized: twerpy Freddy Benson. Every time she babysat he pulled a stunt like this! Her friends at school said it was

because Freddy had a crush on her. She thought he was a grade-A creepazoid.

Lucy slammed the receiver down and sighed heavily. It had not been a good night so far. The Dillon kids had been more mischievous than usual. She had sent them upstairs to get ready for bed, and when she came up she'd found them fooling around in their parents' bedroom. Little Eileen, nine going on nineteen, had been especially sassy. She went to bed clutching some plastic trinket Lucy had been too exasperated to loosen from her tight little fist.

Then the special news report.

Then Freddie the jerk.

It was going to be a long night.

Although she had locked up the downstairs securely, Lucy made another circuit of the rooms, double-checking the doors and windows. She returned to the rec room just in time to hear the second news report on the radio. This time, they were saying what the escaped killer had been put in the state hospital for. It was disgusting. She turned the radio off before the announcer could finish. Surmising that television wouldn't be any better, she pulled out her homework.

She was wrapped up in her efforts to unravel a quadratic equation when a thump sounded upstairs, breaking her concentration.

Eileen, she guessed.

She waited for the sound of footsteps, but they never came.

The house was quiet. Almost too quiet.

RING!

The phone near her elbow jangled, startling her. She laughed nervously when she realized it had made her jump up out of her seat.

Her hand paused over the receiver. If it were Freddy again, picking up the phone would only encourage him. But she couldn't just let the call kick to the answering machine. If Freddy made some stupid remark she couldn't erase, the Dillons would think she was having her friends call her on the job. She could lose work.

It isn't fair! she thought. Biting her lip, she picked up the receiver.

Muffled noises greeted her ear, as though someone had a hand incompletely clamped over the mouthpiece. There seemed to be activity going on, but it was hard to tell what, since a metallic background buzz faded in and out of hearing, distorting sounds from the other end.

Lucy felt her jaws clench. Guess who?

"I know it's you Freddy—and the phone you're using sucks!"

For a second time, she slammed the receiver down.

The nerve of the guy! Lucy felt her anger start to boil. Two calls in fifteen minutes!

She looked at the clock, and saw that it was still not even nine o'clock yet.

Time for reinforcements.

Rummaging through her backpack, Lucy found the security ring she carried with her whenever she went out. It was fully equipped: her house key, a small can of dog repellant—and a whistle. Crossing back over to the phone, she dangled the keyring from her pinky. If Freddy wanted to go to the mat on this, he was going to regret it.

She plopped down in the chair by the phone and tried to go back to her math homework, but with no luck. Waiting for the phone to ring again was like water torture—no matter what you tried to do, all you could think about was when the next ring would come.

Damn you, Freddy!

But it didn't take long. Five, maybe ten minutes. When the phone rang, Lucy put the whistle between her lips and slowly picked up the handset. She heard a sawlike noise that she realized was heavy breathing.

Hesh-sheh. Hesh-sheh. Hesh-sheh.

She paused. Freddy had never done this before. And there was something about the noise that really bothered her. Then, annoyance gave way to a clutching feeling in her chest. The palms of her hands suddenly felt clammy. She felt as though making any movement would attract the attention of something . . . horrible.

Hesh-sheh. Hesh-sheh. Hesh-sheh.

Then a voice that sounded like the voice of every generic psycho she'd heard on a movie soundtrack spoke in a raspy sing-song.

"I'm going to kill the children first . . . then I'm going to get you."

Startled out of her paralysis, Lucy emptied her lungs into the whistle.

Wheeeeeeeeeeeeeeeeeeeeeet!

She blew until she felt her face flush with exertion, then she hung up the phone.

It took Lucy a moment to realize she was trembling, and that her breath was coming in short, shallow bursts. *Damn!* It was as though Freddy had known which buttons to push to scare her—buttons even she didn't know about.

Lucy decided to take the initiative and put a stop to this nonsense before it went any further. Punching up the operator on the phone she complained that she was being harassed on the phone and could they help stop the person who was doing it. The operator put Lucy on hold for several seconds and then a different woman's voice came on the line. She identified herself as a supervisor. They could try to stop the calls, Lucy was told, but they needed her help. From this point on, they would monitor all incoming telephone calls. But could Lucy keep the caller on the phone long enough for them to get a trace? They would then call her back to let her know where the calls were coming from.

Lucy agreed, and sat waiting by the phone.

She waited. And waited. And waited.

The suspense was unbearable, and the longer she sat there the more second thoughts she had. If Freddy didn't call back, she'd look like she was playing pranks herself. Maybe the phone company would wait to call until the Dillons came home, and she'd be the one who got in trouble. Maybe Freddy would get nasty at school.

She reached for the phone to call back the operator and cancel her request.

As though on cue, the phone rang.

This time the breathing on the other end of the line was more rapid and labored.

HeshSHEHheshSHEHheshSHEH.

Then the voice spoke—angrily:

"I'm finished with the children, bitch! Now I'm coming to get YOU!"

That did it. Before he could hang up, Lucy started taunting him. She dared him to come for her. She asked what he was going to do when he got her, and when he gave his sickening answers, she laughed at him.

To his credit, Freddy held his own on the line. It was almost as though he'd been thinking about what he was saying for some time. She'd expected him to sputter and swallow his words, but he seemed to be enjoying the gross detail he used to paint a picture for her. When Lucy thought enough time had passed, she picked up the whistle and put as much lung into it as she could, interrupting him in mid-sentence.

WHHEEEEEEEEEEEEEEEETTTTTT!!!!!

She hoped it ruptured both his eardrums!

It took less than a minute for the operator to call back. She complimented Lucy for doing such a good job. They'd gotten a trace on the phone. The operator provided Lucy with the number, which she wrote down diligently, and the name in which the phone was registered: Thomas Dillon of 12 Parkview Drive.

The pencil she was holding snapped against the pad.

But that was impossible! She was babysitting for Thomas Dillon! She was calling right now from the rec room of the house at 12 Parkview Drive!

The operator paused for several seconds. Then, unemotionally, she informed Lucy that the number was for a cell phone.

There was another pause, before the operator came back on: Just what kind of a prank was Lucy pulling? There was someone at the same house calling on a cell phone. The phone company didn't appreciate—

Lucy let the handset clatter back into the cradle without answering.

Then she remembered Eileen Dillon, her hand wrapped tightly around something she refused to show Lucy. Something small and plastic she had found in her parents' bedroom.

Like a cell phone . . .

It had been the kids all along!

Why, that little . . . !

Lucy stalked over to the staircase and yelled for Eileen to get her little behind downstairs immediately.

But something was already moving quickly at the top of the stairs.

Lucy stared, paralyzed with fear, at a hulking figure in

hospital whites descending the steps. In one hand he brandished a kitchen knife with a cruelly long blade that dripped something dark and viscous from its pointy tip. His other hand gripped Eileen's fist.

Her fist was dripping blood too—*and was still tightly clasped around the cell phone.*

Why the Doctor Went Mad

*Legend: A woman is found dead of fright in her bed, clutch-
ing a telephone in her hand. The phone is a direct line to the
mausoleum of her husband, who had it installed out of fear
that he might be interred alive.*

James Koppel was a highly respected physician with a
degree from a prestigious college and an enviable position as medical examiner for a major metropolitan police
force.

He was also certifiably insane.

Some people thought you'd have to be insane to have
the interest in pathology that Koppel had. In the course of
his work he had seen the worst: gangland-style slayings,
infancticides, suicides of every known type, deaths by
burning and crushing—you name it. But nothing prepared
him for the case that drove him mad.

It began like many of his previous cases, with a phone
call in the middle of the night. The police had been called
by concerned friends to look in on an elderly woman
whose phone line had been surprisingly busy each time
they called for days. When she failed to answer their
knocking, the police broke down the door to her house
and found her inside, dead of apparently natural causes.
Still, there were some irregularities at the crime scene that

warranted the scrutiny of the medical examiner. Would Dr. Koppel come?

The address they gave Koppel was not in one of the usual pest holes where corpses were found at two in the morning. It was in a surprisingly upscale suburban neighborhood.

Koppel was met at the door by a young cop with a sickly look on his face. The doctor figured him for a rookie, since rookies often got assigned to thankless details like this to toughen them up for street duty.

The smell in the house would have been enough to turn anyone's face green. Koppel picked it up just inside the doorway, so it clearly permeated the entire house. The average person feels instinctive revulsion at the smell of death, and Koppel's trained nose told him that whoever the smell was emanating from had been dead at least two, possibly three days. It was November 3. Koppel would want to know the last time anyone had spoken to or otherwise been in contact with the deceased.

The smell grew more pungent as he was escorted up the stairs, and Koppel quickly donned the surgical mask he carried with him on all of his calls. It didn't help much.

In the bedroom where the victim was found, the police looked no better than their partner at the door. Once Koppel saw the corpse, he knew why. Though the face had begun to bloat and mottle from decomposition, he could still make out the look of sheer horror. The woman's eyes, although now sunken and dull, were wide open in fear. Her mouth was stretched in the rictus of a silent scream. In her hand, she still clutched the receiver of the telephone on the table next to the bed.

Koppel performed his preliminary examination silently, doing his best to avoid disturbing the crime scene. There was no sign of foul play or trauma of any sort to the body. An autopsy would be necessary, but Koppel surmised that a heart attack was to blame. The woman hadn't gone easily. The look on her face said that something had literally frightened her to death.

From the state of the tissues and the lividity of parts of the body, Koppel pronounced the time of death some time on the evening of October 31. The officers in the room murmured uneasily, and in response to Koppel's quizzical look one of them reminded him that the 31st was Halloween.

Koppel snorted. He had looked death in the face many times, and his work had made him a skeptic of the first order. He found it hard to believe anyone on police detail could be so superstitious.

Koppel jotted down the date in his pocket notebook. He would need it for the death certificate.

He was informed that the woman was Evelyn Moore, widow of the recently deceased George Moore. That name rang a bell with him, as it surely would have with most doctors in the area. Moore, despite his renown as a wealthy businessman, had been a major hypochondriac. Even the most tolerant practitioners in town had dismissed him from their practices once they learned the seat of his neurosis: he was pathologically afraid of premature burial. Given to fits of prolonged fainting as a young boy, he grew up convinced that someday someone would mistake his unarousability for death and he would awaken inside a coffin. Reassurances that modern mortuary science guaranteed no one would be interred who was not dead only agitated him more. His death fixation was now compounded by the fantasy that he would be powerless to prevent an unwitting mortician from cutting into his living flesh and murdering him on the mortuary slab.

Anticipating the worst, Moore had commissioned a state-of-the-art mausoleum on his family's plot in the local cemetery. Supposedly, it was equipped with conveniences that would help sustain the life of anyone trapped inside it, should he need to avail himself of them. Construction had been completed not a moment too soon, as Moore had keeled over less than a day later at his office. Koppel remembered: he had been the one called to make the official death pronouncement on October 20. The funeral, held two weeks ago, had been a minor media spectacle which he remembered reading about.

Koppel was roused from his thoughts by one of the police officers, who strode into the room to announce that they had traced the last call that had gotten through to Evelyn Moore. It had, indeed, been late on Halloween evening. And it had come from the nearby graveyard: George Moore had apparently paid to have a private line direct to his house installed in the tomb.

Koppel felt his spine turn to ice. Had George Moore somehow been revived from death, escaped his coffin, and called his wife from the phone inside the locked mausoleum?

No! It wasn't possible. This had to be some kind of sick prank. He had signed George Moore's death certificate. Maybe the family had foregone an autopsy. But would someone as neurotic and wealthy as George Moore insist that he not be embalmed?

There was only one way to find out. At James Koppel's instruction, all but two members of the investigative detail piled into a police cruiser and headed for the cemetery.

A storm was breaking in the west, heralded by loud peals of thunder. Though the confines of the car were stuffy Koppel, who sensed the eyes of the other passengers on him, felt uneasily chilled. It was unthinkable that George Moore was alive in his tomb, but if he had somehow managed to endure the last three days Koppel's reputation and career were in jeopardy.

Moore's mausoleum towered like a formidable Gothic

castle above the broken row of headstones that ringed it deep inside the cemetery. The door had been locked and chained, but the police saw no reason to wait for the caretaker to drive over with the appropriate key. Working by the light of a solitary flashlight, they pried the door open with the lug wrench from the cruiser's trunk.

The groaning hinges of the door yielded reluctantly, and a nauseating stench wafting from the blackness on the other side of the doorway set each man back a step. Taking the police flashlight in hand, Koppel walked cautiously through the partial opening.

Several silent seconds later a thunderclap shook the grounds, and a slash of lightning ripped the sky, illuminating the cemetery with a strobe glare of unnaturally sterile light. The police heard Koppel's screams of terror a split second after.

No one would say for sure what it was that Koppel saw inside the tomb. But it was clear to all present that the gibbering maniac who stumbled out the doorway was not the same man who moments before had walked carefully through it.

Koppel is now locked away for his own safety in the psychiatric ward of the city sanitarium, trapped in the private hell of his inarticulable thoughts. It is not possible to know what it is he screams about at 2 A.M. every morning, unless we credit the memory of the officer who claims to have heard the last coherent words he spoke as he emerged from George Moore's tomb.

"He *did* die on October 20. *But he called his wife eleven days later!*"

Ginger Snaps

The Carlson family had just returned home from a night at the movies. Fourteen-year-old Sophie Carlson knew something was wrong the minute she opened her car door. Ginger, their pet German shepherd, wasn't barking. Usually, the dog was well into her chorus of welcoming growls and howls by the time the four of them piled out of the car. In the summertime, with windows open, you could hear Ginger from half a block away.

Tonight, their dark house was perfectly still.

Sophie called her mother's attention to the unusual quiet. Mom assured her Ginger was just asleep.

Ginger!

Sophie called the dog's name as she led her kid sister, Janice, into the house. She waited for the familiar staccato of toenails on linoleum—but there was no response.

Sophie shooed Janice upstairs to her room and went to inspect the kitchen where Ginger's bowls were laid out. Both were as full as they had been when the family left. Flies buzzed the meat chunks in Ginger's food bowl, calling attention to the open kitchen window over the sink. Probably Janice's doing, thought Sophie. She would have to say something to her parents about her sister being totally clueless that you don't leave open windows that don't have screens.

From the second floor, Sophie heard a loud scream.

Janice!

She bounded to the stairs, nearly colliding with her parents as they walked through the front door.

When Sophie reached Janice's room, she screamed too.

Ginger was lying on her side on the floor next to Janice's bed. Her ribs heaved visibly as she labored for breath. She tried to right herself but seemed too weak to roll over from her reclined positioned. The dog's eyes bulged, and her tongue lolled out of her mouth. A small puddle of blood pooled around her spasming jaws. She appeared to be in the throes of some kind of seizure.

Sophie's father swept past the two girls and for the next few moments chaos ensued, with Mr. Carlson trying to coax Ginger back to normalcy, Sophie trying to soothe her bawling sister while crying herself, and Mrs. Carlson frantically placing an emergency call to the veterinarian. The family watched in horror as Ginger's eyes rolled back to white orbs and her lids fluttered closed. Only the ragged heaving of her sides indicated that she was still alive.

Mr. Carlson threw a blanket around Ginger and picked her up as gently as he could. Mrs. Carlson hurriedly instructed Sophie to stay home with Janice until they returned. They piled out of the house with Ginger, and Sophie heard their car spit gravel as her dad peeled out for the vet's.

The sound of Janice's sniveling helped Sophie regain her composure. Crying was for babies, not for a fourteen-year-old.

It took a few minutes for Sophie to calm Janice down. She assured her that Ginger would be all right—although even the mention of the dog's name raised a lump in her own throat.

Knowing that the best thing she could do was get her sister to bed, Sophie volunteered to stay with Janice until she fell asleep. Janice's favorite books were in the shelves by her bed and Sophie began pulling them out as Janice changed into her pajamas.

Creeeaaaak!

The loud noise made Sophie turn.

Janice was slowly donning her nightclothes over by her dresser.

Weird: Sophie could have sworn it sounded like Janice had jumped on the bed.

Eventually, the two of them snuggled side by side, Sophie on top of the covers, Janice beneath them. Sophie breezed through the picture books, picking up the pace as she felt Janice's attention flag. At one point, as she was riffling through the pages, she almost thought she heard a complementary rustling sound somewhere else in the room. But when she stopped, the room was silent, and Janice's mystified look was all the inducement she needed to resume her sibling responsibilities.

In a few more minutes, Janice was lulled to sleep. Sophie had tucked her in gingerly, trying hard to avoid making any loud noise that might awaken her—when the phone rang.

She sprinted for the extension across the hall in her parents' room and answered the phone in a whisper that wouldn't wake Janice up.

It was her mother—but Sophie had never heard her in this state before. Screaming, almost hysterical.

From the corner, Sophie saw movement.

She turned to look into Janice's bedroom. As her mother's words poured out almost unintelligibly, she stared in horrified fascination at the impossible thing she was seeing. In the soft light it appeared to be a snake—a snake with a crimson head. It was rearing up sinuously above Janice's sleeping body. Hovering. As it turned, though, Janice realized there was something protruding from its bloody side.

A thumb.

She made out the shape of something larger wiggling around on the floor.

Something pulling itself out from under the bed!

Sophie's mother was sobbing. Dad and the police were on their way, but she and Janice had to get out of the house—*immediately*. The veterinarian had found what was clogging Ginger's throat.

Four fingers.

She had bitten them off someone.

Maybe a burglar she had surprised.

Whoever it was could still be in the house!

All Mrs. Carlson heard in response was the sound of her two girls screaming.

Legend: A family returns home from a night out and finds their dog nearly asphyxiated from something lodged in its throat. The veterinarian who examines the dog discovers it is choking on the fingers of a burglar the dog surprised inside the house.

Short
Shivers for Long
Car Rides

No matter how scientifically advanced our society becomes, we'll always have superstitions and fears to turn into scary stories. For proof, one need look no further than the number of urban legends that involve automobiles. The cars, trucks, and motorcycles that symbolize our society's technological sophistication often are a magnet for horror.

There are any number of urban legends concerning cars with a "bad" history. In one, a large motor vehicle company is forced to recall a particular batch of dangerously malfunctioning automobiles. No one can figure out why the cars are misbehaving, causing traffic accidents and driver fatalities—until it's discovered that a worker was killed on the assembly line that supplied parts for the autos (or, in the more dramatic version, that a worker fell into the pot of molten steel that eventually was turned into the chassis for the cars). Celebrities, around whom legends naturally grow, figure in a similar type of cursed-car story. Surely you've heard that the succession of drivers who, for novelty sake, bought the car James Dean died in all died in similarly spectacular car crashes. Or that every used car that received a salvaged part from the wreck itself wound up in an accident.

Think of a car as a sort of house on wheels and you begin to appreciate that some of our best urban legends are little more than spooky house stories translated to the open road. The old dark house, with secret passageways that hide a killer who disposes of victims one by one, is the germ of the tale of the killer in the backseat. In this story, a lone driver discovers belatedly (sometimes too belatedly) that his or (usually) her car harbors a man with a knife (sometimes a psychopathic murderer, sometimes a fugitive from the law), who lay in wait at a service station and snuck into the backseat while the driver was gassing up. In the same vein is the legend of the crook who hides under cars in remote corners of the parking lot and disables unsuspecting drivers (again, usually women) by slashing their ankles with a knife as they get in. Likewise, the story of the speeding driver who makes an emergency detour around debris on the road and finds that, in doing so, he or she has driven over three robbers who had placed the debris in the road and were hiding in the grass just off the shoulder, waiting for someone to stop.

An entire tradition of automobile horror stories translates urban legends about kids home alone menaced by psychopaths to a vehicular setting. There are many variations on the classic "tale of the hook," but all generally involve a teenage boy and girl forced home from lovers lane after hearing a radio report of an escaped criminal with a hook for a hand, who later find a bloody hook dangling from the outside of their car door. In a grislier version of this story, a boy and his girlfriend hear the radio report and set out to leave, only to discover that the car's engine is dead. The boy goes for help, telling the girl to lock the door and not leave the car for any reason until his return. All night, while the boy is gone, the girl is terrorized by the sound of steady tapping on the roof of the car. The next morning, she is rescued by police—and sees the butchered corpse of her boyfriend hanging from branches of a tree above the car, his blood still spattering the roof.

The biggest threat to drivers in auto urban legends tends to be hitchhikers, who prey on our natural desire to play the Good Samaritan. The tale of the cross-dressing hitchhiker is one of the more benign of its type: it tells of a man who dresses like a woman to get picked up by drivers (usually sympathetic women), and whose cover is blown by his abnormally hairy arms. The few overtly supernatural automobile legends are mostly hitchhiker variants. There are multiple versions of the tale of the vanishing hitchhiker, but all involve a mysterious hitchhiker who disappears from the car after directing the driver to a specific location. Later, it's revealed that the hitchhiker was actually the ghost of someone killed on the road. In a more diabolical version, a driver on a deserted stretch of road picks up a lone hitchhiker who appears to have crippled legs. Once inside the car, the passenger is found to have cloven hooves for feet. It's hardly surprising, then, that there are also tales of a hitchhiker who shows up at multiple locations along a driver's route and turns out to be death incarnate.

In the world of urban legends, the car is simply a passport for travel in *terra* (or *terror*) *incognita*.

Stay Away from Wilson Drive!

Legend: A driver stops to pick up a hitchhiker along a deserted stretch of road. When asked where he or she is heading, the hitchhiker only points down the road and is uncommunicative the rest of the trip. When the driver reaches the passenger's destination, it is discovered that the hitchhiker has vanished from the car.

In the low beams of Janine Winslow's headlights, the dense fog shrouding Wilson Drive looked like an encroaching army of ghostly beings with grotesquely shifting faces. Even the hum of her car's motor seemed muffled by the cottony tendrils that probed and caressed her vehicle.

She was just rounding one of the road's sinuous bends when a little girl appeared from out of nowhere, right in front of her car. Janine braked hard and felt the car slew around on the mist-slicked pavement. There was no way she could avoid hitting the girl! She braced herself for the sickening thud of impact. . . .

Incredibly, it never came. The tires squealed in resistance against the grade of the road, and the car skidded to a halt. Janine sat with her head pressed against the steering wheel, breathing in short, shallow gasps. After a moment, she turned her head toward the driver's window.

She screamed at the horribly distorted face that looked in at her.

At least that's what it appeared to be, until she gathered her wits and realized it was the face of the little girl she had nearly hit. Hands cupped around the face, as someone would do to get a better peek inside the darkened window, had given it a monstrously abnormal shape.

When Janine opened her car door to scold her, she realized that the girl's agitated expression had contributed to her eerie appearance. From what Janine could make of her features in the dim dome light of the car, she was a fair-haired child of seven or eight, and her face and clothes were caked with streaks of grime or mud. She had been out for some time.

"Please, please, please, take me home! I'm scared!" she wailed. Her cry was so heartbreaking it thwarted any idea Janine had of scolding the girl for nearly causing an accident.

Instinctively, Janine opened the rear door of the car, and the little girl piled in. Only after several queries was Janine able to discover that the girl lived farther up Wilson Drive. Her pitiful snivels were punctuated with whimpers and whines that frustrated any attempt at finding out what her name was, or what she was doing on the road at this time of evening.

Only as Janine was buckling herself into the driver's seat did it register that the little girl had no coat on, just a denim dress that couldn't have offered much warmth. Janine passed back the cardigan sweater she had shucked into the passenger seat before heading home from the office, and felt an icy chill where the child's skin made contact with her. The girl had to be freezing to make Janine herself shiver so. Janine fully intended to give the girl's parents a piece of her mind on their negligent care of their daughter.

The trip along Wilson Drive was miserable, with Janine trying to concentrate on the road before her while murmuring soothing reassurances to her passenger. The complete absence of other cars on the road compounded her uneasiness. At one point she snuck a peak into the rearview mirror to see how the girl was doing.

And she could not make out the girl's quivering shape!

Certain it had to be a trick of the light and bad weather, Janine rubbed her cloudy rearview mirror, but the crunch of gravel that indicated the car was veering onto the shoulder forced her attention back to the road.

She heard a sniffle from the backseat, and realized how silly her fears were.

Almost as suddenly as the girl had appeared in the road, a house materialized out of the haze on the right side. The girl's cries turned to sounds of relief.

Janine's headlights picked up a dented silvery mailbox jutting off the shoulder and she maneuvered her car up the gravel drive. She saw a front porch light gleaming a sickly yellow in the soupy atmosphere, and smelled the pungent woodsmoke of a fire as she got out of the car.

Janine reached in to help the little girl out of the back.

But her hand met only with air.

Thinking she had perhaps frightened the girl by her abrupt movements, Janine crouched down to peer into the backseat.

The car was completely empty.

A panicky feeling clutched at her throat. Had the girl left the car from the other side? No! She would have heard the car door slam. She patted the seat where the girl had sat, only to find it cold—almost as though it had been vacant all along.

Unnerved, Janine stumbled up the flagstone sidewalk to the porch of the house and pounded on the screen door. Her urgent blows eventually persuaded a startled man and woman inside to open the door and listen to her as she blurted out her story.

As shocking as the evening had been, Janine was completely unprepared for the tirade that followed from the man on the other side of the screen. He accused her of having a sick sense of humor and berated her behavior. Wasn't it bad enough he and his wife had buried their only child when she was struck by a car on Wilson Drive five years before? Now, on the anniversary of her death, they had to deal with some idiot cruelly reminding them of their tragedy.

The rush of air from the slammed front door was like a hard slap against Janine's face.

She awoke the next morning still shaken, and not at all sure how she had gotten home. As she pulled herself together for her trip to the office, she realized that the sweater in which she had put her pass and office keys was nowhere to be found. A search of her car turned up nothing.

With mounting dread, she recalled handing the sweater to the little girl on Wilson Drive. Her memory of that icy touch brought goose bumps.

No doubt, she would find her sweater along the road where she had stopped her car. Or possibly in the driveway of the house she had stopped at.

Gathering her courage, she left to retrace her steps of the previous evening.

The police found Janine Winslow just before noon that day, wandering dazedly in the charred ruins of a house on Wilson Drive. It was recognizable only by the dented silver mailbox at the roadside. It's from them that we know the story of her return to Wilson Drive and her search for the misplaced sweater.

Try as they might, the police could not comfort Janine. They told her how a young girl had been killed on Wilson Drive after having left her house and lost her way in the dense fog of an October night. And they told her how, four years later, the house of the girl's grief-stricken parents had burned to the ground. They told her that no one had lived on Wilson Drive since, because of the unhealthy atmosphere that seemed to hover over the road, and seemed to permeate the fogs which were always thicker on Wilson Drive in October, the month the young girl was killed.

The police were very patient in their explanations. They are always patient when speaking to people who accidentally travel Wilson Drive in the month of October. But they can't explain everything.

For instance, they could not explain to Janine why she found her missing sweater, with her office keys and pass, dirty but intact, hanging on the back of a child's chair buried in the charcoal rubble of a house that had supposedly burned down four years earlier.

Backseat Driver

S andy Parker was traveling west from Chicago to visit family. She had just gassed her car up inside the Nebraska border when she noticed the headlights in her rearview mirror. She thought it was a little unusual, since the sun had to be shining right in the driver's eyes—as it was in hers. The highway would be well lit for at least another hour.

Sandy guessed the owner was the cautious driver type. Probably some old geezer with bad eyes who needed the dashlights on to see how fast he was going.

Maybe the car was one of those new ones whose lights automatically went on the second the ignition turned over. Everyone claimed that kind of lighting system made it safer to drive at twilight, since that was when the visibility of cars without lights was poorest.

Yeah, right! Try telling that to someone getting blinded doubly, by the setting sun up front *and* a pair of headlights from behind.

Sandy looked at the road and sighed. It was a two-lane highway through the cornfields. According to her map, she would be on it for a good fifty miles. That meant that unless the car behind exited she'd be dealing with his glaring headlights until close to sundown.

When she looked again in the rearview mirror, she saw

that he was gaining on her, at a moderate speed. Her own speedometer hovered at 70. This guy was trucking at 75 at least, in defiance of the posted speed limits. With luck, he'd pass her without even breaking stride.

But no such luck. The guy pulled up behind her—and stayed there. He was maybe two car lengths back, or about five too short for the speed they were traveling. His lights, which a half mile away had been pesky flickers in her mirror, were now obnoxious flares of fire that made her eyes smart when she flicked them toward her mirror.

She tried to get a good look at the car in her mirror. It was bright red—*Naturally!*—and had the look of a Camaro. Definitely a shitkicker car. Probably being driven by some pimply-faced teen who'd brag about intimidating an out-of-stater in a Toyota like it was the high point of his pathetically unfulfilled life.

Sandy tried to twist the mirror to reflect the light straight back into the driver's eyes, but the angle didn't allow for it.

When she spot-checked her mirror again, she saw the red car flash its high beams.

High-low. High-low. The universal signal that translated as: "Eat my dust! I'm passing!"

Hallelujah! Sandy did exactly what she remembered the driver's manual telling her she should do under the circumstances. She pulled slightly to the right, to give the car all the room it needed, and cut her speed graciously by five miles per hour, just to hasten his passage.

The car behind her did the same. And it saluted her again with flashing lights.

High-low. High-low.

Sandy gritted her teeth.

What the hell do you want?

She lifted her foot from the accelerator and with the corner of her eye watched the speedometer drop another five miles per hour.

In the rearview mirror the gap between her and the pursuing car closed quickly as her reduced speed caught the driver unexpectedly. The edge of the car's bumper dropped out of frame, then yo-yoed back in again as the driver let up on the accelerator.

And he flicked his highs and lows again!

Well pass, dammit!

But this guy didn't want to pass. He wanted to play cat and mouse!

For the first time that evening Sandy felt a twinge of uneasiness. This was a lonely stretch of road and she was a solitary female driver. She didn't like the idea of playing games with some cretin who would probably consider running her off the road all part of the day's fun.

Sandy took her foot off the gas and watched her speedometer drop steadily: 65, 60, 55, 50, 45, 40.

The red Camaro dropped back accordingly, keeping perfect pace with her.

All the while the car's headlights bored intensely into her from behind.

For a moment Sandy thought about pulling off to the shoulder, or letting her car slow to a complete stop. Then she thought better of it. Maybe that was what the guy wanted. Maybe he was trying to corral her, to trick his way around her so that he could force her to a stop and rob her.

Or worse.

This just couldn't be happening!

Where the hell had the guy come from?

Sandy glanced hopefully at her odometer, then silently cursed. She still had another 35 miles to go before her exit. She wondered if it might not be smart to turn off the road the first opportunity she got, to shake the red car. But the driver probably knew this area better than she did, and once off the highway she would have no idea of where to go or what to do. Instead of 50 miles to civilization, it could be another 100. This part of the state was all farmland.

The sun was dipping below the horizon, but still blazing incandescently in the late afternoon sky. Heat waves rising off the road so distorted perception of distance that Sandy almost didn't notice the car approaching from the opposite direction.

Salvation!

She flicked her lights on and off repeatedly.

There was no response from the approaching car.

The irony of her predicament struck her: *He probably thinks I'm telling him to put his lights on!*

She resorted to the tactics of her pursuer instead: *High-low. High-low. High-low.*

The approaching car responded in type: *high-low, high-low, high-low!*

Sandy pounded the wheel with her right fist in frustration.

This is not a joust, you stupid redneck!

As Sandy realized that the rapidly approaching car was not going to stop, she bumped her high beams on full and pressed all the weight she could on her car horn.

The approaching car also clicked on his highs and flew by, the driver sticking his arm out the window and flipping her off with the middle finger.

No! No! No! No! No!

Sandy realized she was sobbing as her final chance for help sped past. She saw his trail of dust billow behind her in the rearview mirror—

—that part of the mirror that wasn't dominated by the pursuing Camaro.

She bit down hard on her lip, trying to regain her composure. This couldn't be happening! It reminded her of a television movie she'd seen where some luckless guy in a beat-up old car was forced to play road games with a scary son-of-a-bitch in an oil tanker who hung on his tail for the whole trip.

She couldn't remember if the guy lived at the end of the movie or not. . . .

The sun was halfway below the horizon now, and the landscape zipping by was getting darker, throwing up looming shadows. Sandy feared the coming night. Once she had to put her lights on, her room to maneuver with any confidence would be limited to the area she could see with her headlights. Her options for escape were beginning to evaporate.

The red Camaro seemed attuned to her concern. It pulled out from behind her into the lane for oncoming traffic and began to accelerate.

Ohmigod. He's going to try to cut me off!

But the Camaro didn't do that. Once it pulled even with her, it stayed there—matching her speed, traveling in perfect tandem.

Sandy accelerated.

So did the Camaro.

She eased off.

So did the Camaro.

Sandy began to whimper under her breath. The Camaro was playing chicken with her. She knew the driver was trying to catch her attention. She was terrified to look at him—but she did.

In the waning light, she saw a hulking figure in the front seat of the car. His features were shrouded in darkness. But the pointing motion he was making with his hand, flinging it out toward her, was easy to understand:

He wants me to pull over!

Sandy nearly stood on the accelerator. With a lurch, her car kicked into high gear. She pulled ahead, but only momentarily. The Camaro sped up to run neck and neck with her again. And now the guy inside was furious. He wasn't pointing anymore: he was making a chopping motion with his hand.

Sandy knew what he was going to chop if he got the chance.

A red light on her dash flashed, and Sandy knew her radiator was due to overheat if she kept this torture on her car up much longer.

Both Sandy and the Camaro had been so desperately trying to catch or escape each other's attention that neither noticed the vehicle traveling in the eastbound lane.

An eighteen-wheeler. Heading right for the Camaro. And with Sandy in the other lane, the guy didn't have many choices for where to go.

The truck's steam horn blasted, but there was no way the Camaro would have time to pull out of danger's way. Sandy heard the car's brakes shriek, and a crunch of metal.

She prayed that it had been crushed like a bug on a windshield.

It hadn't, though. Through her side window, she saw the car shoot off into a cornfield, its passenger door nearly torn off. Over her shoulder, there was a whine of hydraulics. The truck was braking hard to a full stop.

Yes! Yes! Yes!

Sandy pumped her fist in the air in a gesture of victory. Tears of relief rolled down her cheeks as she offered up a prayer for her incredible good fortune. Keeping her foot steady on the accelerator, she gleefully rode into the sunset, putting all the distance she could between her and the two vehicles fast receding in her mirror.

The driver of the Camaro did not share her elation. When the police came to retrieve him from the field an hour later, they found him pressing his blood-smeared face against the steering wheel in total dejection. Later, he would tell the police how he had been following the woman from the gas station. She had gassed her car up ahead of his. He had tried every tactic he could once she was on the road to get her stop.

She couldn't have known that while she was inside paying the cashier, he had seen a man sneak into the backseat of her car.

And that man was carrying an axe.

Legend: A woman driver tries to elude a car that persistently pursues her. Later, it's discovered that the driver of the pursuing car was actually trying to warn her that an armed man had snuck into the backseat of her car at the last gas station she stopped at.

One More

Legend: A woman has a recurring dream of a deathly figure that beckons her aboard a vehicle with the assurance that there's "room for one more." It proves to be a premonition of an accident she narrowly escapes.

It was twilight, and Sharon Byrne was running down a dirt road, dressed in a flimsy gossamer gown not of this century that made her feel extremely vulnerable. The landscape around her was desolate and blighted. Clumps of overgrown weeds, bleached a sallow yellow, choked the ground. They were punctuated by pools of stagnant water that gave off miasmas of noxious vapors. She gagged with each panting breath. Rocks that lined the roadway looked like nothing so much as aged, deformed human skulls. The dust her footsteps kicked up only reinforced her feeling that this was a dead and decaying world.

Behind her a full moon rose, looking wan and sterile. Before her, she saw the dying sun fast disappearing behind a range of blackened mountains too distant for her to reach before the world turned dark. She was running toward the sun—

—and, she realized, running from something behind her that was frightening her to death!

BadaBUMP! BadaBUMP! BadaBUMP! BadaBUMP!

She heard the rapid pounding of hoofbeats. Someone on horseback was pursuing her—and gaining ground!

Sharon pushed herself to the limits of her endurance to flee the approaching sound. Her lungs felt seared by the dry, fetid air. Her legs and arms burned from what felt like acid under her skin.

But no matter how hard she tried, she had the terrifying dream sense of running in place, exerting herself futilely to outrun the inescapable.

BadaBUMP! BadaBUMP! BadaBUMP! BadaBUMP!

The sounds were almost at her heels! She knew she did not dare turn around to look at what was chasing her, for fear of losing balance and stumbling to the roadway! Her breath began to come in ragged sobs, and still the sounds came nearer, and nearer.

BADABUMP! BADABUMP! BADABUMP! BADABUMP!

The pounding hoofbeats were so loud that they seemed to be coming from within her head as well as outside, crushing her body with each beat. Sharon closed her eyes, bracing for the impact of razor-sharp hooves sure to run her down. She felt herself pitch forward to the ground.

When she hazarded a look back over her shoulder, there was nothing to see but a cloud of settling dust. Then the snort of a horse startled her and she whipped her head forward.

Somehow, the carriage had gotten in front of her to block her path!

It was an awesome spectacle: a huge coach, solid black in color and trim, drawn by six tremendous steeds who struck sparks as their flinty hooves pawed the ground. The horses were also pitch black, save for their malignant eyes, which gleamed a fiery red in the fading sunlight. Their breath steamed in the cooling air, and it had the smell of smoke.

On top of the carriage sat a figure in a black cloak, a

cowl pulled up to conceal his face. He clutched a long black whip in one hand and held the reins in the other. Something about him inspired instinctive revulsion in Sharon.

From her sprawl on the ground, she looked up at the window of the carriage and saw faces behind it. Agonized faces of people banging hands on the glass, pleading with her to help them and warning her away.

The faces of the damned!

She looked back to the driver and saw him leaning down. The arm he extended was skeletally thin, and when his hood pulled aside she saw a death's head inside.

No need to run, m'lady, he cooed in a raspy voice. There's room for one more.

For the third time that month, Sharon awoke, howling in terror, with the sound of those words echoing in her ears.

She sought advice from everyone she knew about the meaning of her dream. Her mother told her it was proof she felt guilty about something. Her therapist asked her if a loved one had died recently. Her boyfriend was too preoccupied with the football game on television to even respond.

The sleepless nights she endured after these dreams were ruining her life, sapping her strength to work and fatiguing her to the point where she sometimes made dangerous mistakes. One morning after her nightmare, as she was crossing a city street in an insomniac stupor, she was almost run down by a cab she failed to see.

It was another morning after the nightmare that Sharon was waiting for her bus to work and noticed as it approached that it looked different. Nothing she could put her finger on; just the sense that there was something odd about the vehicle.

As the bus pulled alongside the curb, Sharon got onto the back of the line and queued up to the door. She was almost on board when she heard the bus driver announce:

Room for one more!

Sharon halted, her foot in mid-air above the step, and stared in fright at the driver just as he turned his head back from his survey of the bus's interior. She saw a wizened man, whose body was thin and sickly, but whose eyes overpowered her with manic intensity. She knew where she had seen those features before.

Sharon felt as though she were back in her dream, powerless to make any forward movement, even as the driver beckoned her with a crooked finger. The noises all around her sounded as though they were filtering through thick insulation, and the colors took on the tinted look of old film stock.

The spell was broken by a frenzied commuter, who rushed onto the bus from behind her. The doors closed with a pneumatic hiss, and the bus drove off, the driver staring at her with a sardonic grin on his face.

The next morning, the tragedy was emblazoned across the front page of all the newspapers. A bus packed with commuters had lost control shortly after Sharon's stop and had run off a bridge onto the roadbed below. Everyone on the bus, including the driver, had died in the fiery wreckage.

An icy chill spread along Sharon's spine as she realized the import of the news story. Her dreams had not been the fevered fancies of an excited imagination! They had been warnings. She could have been on that bus. But she had known not to board it.

Sharon knew she should be exhilarated that she had cheated death, but she couldn't summon the enthusiasm. She felt edgy and apprehensive, the way she felt when walking past a dark alleyway by herself late at night.

She cleaned up her breakfast dishes and dressed for her job in a daze. She hoped for nothing less than a solid day of demanding work in which she could completely immerse herself.

She was just locking her door when she heard the apartment building's elevator *ping* open on her floor. It was an old twelve-story building, and she knew the next elevator could take forever.

She pleaded with whoever was in the elevator to hold the door, and sprinted. As she flew through the doors, she saw that the only other occupant was the elderly lift operator. He seemed shrunken and insubstantial in his baggy uniform. As the doors closed inescapably behind her, and the long descent began, he turned his sneering face upon her and chortled in a sandpapery voice:

No need to run, lady. There's room for one more!

Death Takes Its Toll

Legend: As a prank, medical students leave parts of their ca-davers in the outstretched hands of toll collectors.

J ames Myers wasn't always the taciturn man he is today. He developed his sour disposition only after working a few weeks at the bridge tollbooth.

There was no reason for James not to like his new job— at least at first. The work wasn't too taxing, the pay was good, and the hours weren't intolerable. James worked the late shift from 10 P.M. to 6 in the morning, when traffic was its slowest and it was easy to catch up on his reading in the long intervals between cars. It cost exactly a dollar to cross the bridge, so usually it wasn't even necessary for him to look up from his book when the cars passed through. He'd just stick his hand out mechanically, take the bill handed to him, and deposit it in his cash drawer as the car accel-erated off across the river.

The job was so easy James couldn't figure out why his predecessor had given it up—and so suddenly! James had spent a few minutes of his first shift cleaning out the per-sonal knickknacks the guy had left in the booth, a sure sign of a rapid departure. When he asked his supervisor what to do with them, he'd been instructed to throw them out—not likely the guy would ever come back for them. James was going to ask what had happened but stopped when he saw the supervisor's scowl. He wasn't about to risk losing a cushy job just because he was curious.

James found out what he wanted—and perhaps more than he needed—to know on Halloween.

It was a surprisingly warm night, and a bank of fog had risen from the river to envelop the toll plaza. Although the booths were separated by only a few feet, James found that the murk made it difficult to see the other toll collectors working around him. The lights on the booths gave the swirling vapors an otherworldly glow that only intensified his feelings of being cut off from the world.

James was so engrossed in a paperback horror novel about a mad doctor that he didn't hear the car pull up in his lane until it was flush with his booth. Without paying attention, James stuck his hand out. He felt the familiar flick of a bill in the crease of his palm—and something else.

Something hard and chitinous—like insect legs.

James looked over and was startled to see a pale-faced vampire tickling his hand with two-inch long nails, crusted with graveyard dirt.

Three more peered out at him from the car windows.

James jerked his hand back in revulsion.

Then the vampires began to laugh—and soon, he was laughing with them.

Kids!

Probably from one of the city colleges—on their way to a costume party in the suburbs.

Ever the good sport, James hooked his fingers into fang-like prongs to take the bill from them.

There were a few more cars of Halloween revelers that evening, but by 2 A.M. the traffic came separated by spans of fifteen to twenty minutes. The fog had grown thicker, and it seemed to blanket noise outside the booth, giving the night an eerie stillness.

James was just beginning to wonder if he would handle another vehicle that evening when a car pulled to a screeching halt in his lane and made him jump with surprise inside the booth. Through the fog-shrouded window, he could make out someone wearing a slouch hat that concealed his face. He clutched a dollar in a hand that barely extended beyond the cuff of the cloak he wore. Upset at being startled, James took his time reaching for the bill. The second it was in his hand, though, the car peeled out past the booth, swirling a cloud of burned rubber into the fog and setting off the alarm James hadn't had time to release before passing the car through.

James swung out of his booth to stare in disbelief at taillights disappearing rapidly into the fog.

It was a moment before he felt the cold sensation in his hand.

Looking down, James was aghast to see that he held the driver's dollar-pinching hand in his own!

His mind raced to convince him that it was just a sculpted Halloween prop, but when he turned the hand toward him, he saw the all-too-real cross section of bone, gristle, and liquefying flesh at the wrist.

With a shriek, James hurled the hand from him. It hit the booth across from his and rebounded back into the lane. James tripped on the curb trying to regain the safety of his booth and found himself only inches away from the disgusting artifact. He could have sworn he saw the thing start crawling away from him on its own, like a crippled spider lurching forward on only five legs—but would later be persuaded by his fellow workers that it was just an illusion caused by his trying to push himself backward, away from it.

They managed to calm James down in the supervisor's booth in the time it took for the authorities to show. A smirking young trooper walked in holding the hand nonchalantly and offered only a single word of explanation as he tossed the grisly trophy on the supervisor's desk:

Pickled.

James was informed that it was a common prank of medical students in the city to steal parts of the cadavers kept in the gross anatomy lab and drop them at the tollbooth. It tended to happen more in the fall, when new students were most likely to be dared to do it.

James was lucky, they told him. The guy who had manned the booth before he was hired had been handed . . . well, something that had given him good reason to walk.

James kept his job at the bridge tollbooth, but he's not as happy-go-lucky as he once was. On foggy October nights especially, he looks anxious and wary of the cars that pull into his booth.

And he *never* laughs when people call his late work hours "the graveyard shift."

Roadside Stop

The highway motel Edna Chase pulled her car up in front of looked no different from any other she had ever stayed in: low barracks-style units stretching the length of the poorly tended asphalt parking lot, maroon paint faded and peeled by the elements, a general atmosphere of dinginess.

If she were traveling by herself, she might have driven on to the next large town, but her mother was with her, and both of them were beginning to wilt in the late afternoon heat. A night's rest, no matter how plain the accommodations, would refresh them for the rest of their trip.

The front office was open but unoccupied. Edna slapped the bell and heard the tinny ring swallowed up by the stillness. It summoned an official-looking man from the back. He had a haggard look, and the sport coat he wore had clearly seen better days. Reflexively, the man set about registering them.

Edna tried to engage him in small talk, but her comments about the weather and the road got her no more than a series of grunts in reply. Once she and her mother had signed the register, the man slapped a keyring with a number on it down on the counter.

Room 13.

The room proved to be the last of the units, and was reached by turning at the end of the long row of rooms toward the back of the lot. It hadn't been aired for some time, and had a stuffiness that the ancient air-conditioner could not alleviate. Edna briefly considered asking for another room; she and her mother were clearly the only guests, and no doubt would have had their choice of units. But she guessed that the other rooms wouldn't be any better, and this one afforded a little more privacy.

Edna volunteered to pick up provisions from nearby stores while her mother unpacked. It wasn't until she reached her car that she realized she had forgotten to take the room key with her. Not that it really mattered.

She wasn't more than twenty minutes at a nearby convenience store. Cradling two bags of groceries, she nudged the car door shut with her knee and walked to the end of the row of rooms, intending to knock for entrance with her elbow. She turned the corner—

—and nearly pitched over the rim of a weed-covered foundation. Before her stretched an expanse of vacant lot. Room 13 was not there!

Had she accidentally gone to the wrong end of the building?

No—when she backtracked she saw the number 12 on the room she had just passed.

It wasn't possible that she had driven to the wrong motel. She had seen nothing else resembling this place on her way to the store.

Edna heard a crunch of gravel behind her. Whirling in panic, she stepped right into a pair of clutching hands!

She screamed and flailed, groceries flying.

When she regained her composure, she saw that she was being held by a young man in a polo shirt who had a very concerned look on his face. He explained that he had seen her prowling around the parking lot. Did she need a room to stay in?

In the front office, Edna anxiously explained that she

and her mother checked in less than an hour before. The young man expressed his surprise, since he hadn't checked in anyone for a room in nearly a week. He showed Edna the dated ledger.

Her and her mother's signatures were nowhere to be seen.

In a quavering voice, Edna insisted that she and her mother had been registered and given the key to room 13.

There was no room 13, the man said calmly. There had been, once. But a problem had led to room 13 being torn down—ten years before!

He jerked his thumb over his shoulder, indicating the Peg-Board on the wall behind him. Nails held the keyrings for twelve rooms. There was a nail hole under the number 13, but no nail or keyring.

Bewildered, Edna glanced around the office, looking for some clue to support her claim. It was then that she spied a framed picture of a man and woman on the ledge behind the desk.

That was him! That was the man who had checked her and her mother in.

Impossible, the clerk said in solemn tone. The man in the picture was long dead.

He was the former owner of the motel.

The clerk's father.

Ten years ago, in the heat of a midsummer day, he had gone berserk, and killed a female guest and himself.

In room 13!

Legend: A woman briefly leaves her mother in a room at a roadside motel. When she returns, she finds that the room is no longer there and no one can remember checking them in.

Ḧook Ending

Ṫhe radio was full of news reports about a killer who had escaped from the local insane asylum. The man had killed two guards while making his getaway. It was easy for him. He was crazy—and he had a hook instead of a hand at the end of his left arm. Rumor had it that the guy had hacked off his own hand years before to slip out of a pair of handcuffs. At the asylum they had outfitted him with a rusty old hook that had been taken off a dead inmate.

The asylum had made a big mistake.

Terry Jackson had made a big mistake too. He was playing soft music on his car's cassette deck that evening to get his girlfriend Lisa in a romantic mood. So the couple never heard the news reports about the escaped killer.

Terry had been dating Lisa for more than two weeks, and that was long enough for him to be more serious than he'd been with his previous girlfriends. He had a special evening planned out for them—a private one, far away from the usual hangouts. The location was a secluded clearing in the woods, at the crest of a hill about a mile off the main road. The only way to get to it was by a pair of tire tracks worn into the underbrush for the whole distance.

Terry had just snaked his arm around Lisa's shoulders when a noise louder than the night creatures' symphony of sound knifed through the darkness.

Crack! Crack!

The chirps and chitters of the nocturnal animals stopped suddenly. Lisa lifted her head from Terry's shoulder to listen. Sensing her nervousness, Terry assured her that it was just the sound of branches falling from a tree. They sometimes did that in the forest, where the limbs could grow too big for the trees to support their weight.

When Terry started kissing Lisa, he was oblivious to everything else except the feeling of her skin beneath his fingers and a growing sense of warmth. So he wasn't even aware of anything wrong until he felt Lisa pull sharply away from him, asking what that noise was.

Click-click. Click-click. Click-click.

It sounded to Terry like crab pincers clicking together—which was ridiculous, considering where they were and how big the crab would have to be to make so loud a noise.

They heard the sound again.

Click-click. Click-click. Click-click.

It was closer this time. Then a light breeze blew through the window, stirring leaves across the rear window. Terry told Lisa to relax. It was just the sound of a twig slapping against the trunk. This wasn't a scene from one of those stupid horror movies they watched at the drive-in, he reminded her. It was just a date, and they were both supposed to be enjoying it.

Terry directed Lisa's attention through the windshield. There was a break at the top of trees, and a full moon was rising. This was what he had wanted her to see.

Screeeeeeeeeeeeeeeeeee!

A long scratching noise sounded outside Lisa's window and Terry felt her harden like a rock in his embrace. She was frightened and demanded to be taken home. Terry's rage finally bubbled over. Heedless of what the surrounding trees might do to his car, he revved the car's engine, slewed the vehicle around, then peeled out back down the bumpy tire ruts, sending rocks and dirt flying beneath his wheels. All the way back to Lisa's house he berated her for acting like such a baby.

When Terry pulled into the driveway of her house, Lisa barely waited for him to stop the car before wrenching the door open to run inside. Terry's mind was already on what he would do for the rest of the evening when he heard her scream.

He saw Lisa staring in horror at the door on the passenger side, her mouth wide open but still too small for the sound she made.

Terry was out of the driver's seat in a second, running around to her side of the car. What he saw there made no sense:

A deep gouge in the finish of the passenger side of the car, scoring it from tail to front door—

—and dangling from the door handle, a rusty hook ending in a bloody stump!

Legend: Unaware that a psychotic killer with a hook for a hand has escaped from a nearby asylum, a young boy and girl drive off into the woods to go necking. But the girl is unnerved by the strange night sounds she hears outside and the boy finally drives her home in frustration. When the girl opens the car door, she finds a bloody hook dangling from the handle.

Frights for the Christmas Fireside

Christmas, that most festive of holidays—a time for terror? You wouldn't think so. But Christmas, more than most other holidays, comes with a closetful of traditions steeped in superstitions and beliefs of less enlightened times. Consider that the communal yuletide spirit of goodwill toward all evolved in part to repel forces of evil thought to lie in wait for individuals in the cold and dark at the year's end, and the gloomier aspects of the holiday's cheeriest customs make sense.

The dark side of Christmas tradition tends to focus on the benefits that you do *not* receive if you fail to follow ritual correctly. Take the burning of the yule log, a ritual that protects your home from fire and lightning and brings good fortune for the year to come—*only* if you follow stipulations as detailed as a pharmaceutical packaging insert. You don't buy your yule log; you cut it down yourself, preferably a tree on your own property. You have to light it from the fragment of last year's log kept tucked under your bed, and woe betide you if it doesn't catch fire on the first attempt. You can sit back and enjoy the fire, but it has to stay lit for twelve hours—all night—and no one can stir the embers during the Christmas meal. Should anyone who passes before the light of the fire cast a headless shadow—well, you won't have to worry about buying that person a Christmas gift next year.

Many people decorate their homes with Christmas trees and boughs. Bring the greenery into your house before Christmas Eve, however, and you're not only asking to be a lightning rod for evil spirits, you're jeopardizing the return of foliage at winter's end. Similar repercussions await the person foolish enough to cut down a holly bush or bring ivy into the home. Even mistletoe, that most romantic of plants, has its cautionary side. Leave it hanging in the house all year round, and replace it only at the next yuletide season, or you'll lose your protection against witchcraft. Dispose of your Christmas greenery with the utmost care, by burning, and on a specific day (generally February 1). If you experience misfortunes in the following year, they're the work of goblins, whose number corresponds to the number of needles left in your house from the Christmas tree.

Certain things are never done outside the yuletide season unless you wish to incur the luck of Jonah: you can eat mince pies only between Christmas Eve and Twelfth Night, and you *never* sing Christmas carols at any time other than the holiday season. Other things must never be done *during* Christmastime: overhearing farm animals on Christmas Eve, when they are temporarily granted the power to speak in a human tongue, is a death sentence.

The dangers of not following these yuletide traditions to the letter of the law are implicit in our best-known modern Christmas legends. You have to be sure you know what's in the first boxes under your tree. You should only let bona fide Santas into your house, and only through a chimney that you know is clear. Know where you got your Christmas tree from, and be mindful of the ornaments and decorations you use to deck your halls. To do any less is to invite a fate as unspeakable as any whispered in the traditional ghost story.

Ɓe Sees You When You're Sleeping

Legend: An escapee from the state hospital eludes police on Christmas Eve by dressing up as Santa Claus.

It was Christmas Eve, and one of the ice storms so common to the season had taken out the power as it whipped through the countryside. The ice capped a blizzard from the day before that had blanketed the countryside with over a foot of snow.

Elizabeth Trent and her four-year-old son, Timothy, lived in an old farmhouse just outside city limits, and she was still waiting for her electricity to come back on. Her phone was dead as well. A limb on one of the large trees near the house had cracked under the strain of its icy burden and taken the lines out with it. Looking out through her front window, across the dunes of snow glistening in the evening sun, Elizabeth felt completely cut off from the world.

Crack!

The sound of ice splintering from the roof and crashing to the glazed snow beneath sounded like a gunshot in the quiet outside her window. From the corner of her eye, she thought she glimpsed a flash of color through the window, but when she craned her neck to investigate, she saw Timmy standing in the kitchen doorway. All during the past few days, he had expressed his wish to see Santa Claus. Now, with the night before

Christmas fast approaching, his antsiness was a tangible electric current.

Out in the living room, the tree was still only half-decorated, a casualty of the morning's power outage. With an eye toward giving her son an outlet for his nervous energy and helping to tire him out for the evening, Elizabeth lit candles around the room and persuaded Timmy to help her finish the trimming.

They were just beginning to hook ornaments on the branches when she heard a muffled crunching sound. Fearing Timmy had crushed one of the glass ornaments beneath his bare feet, Elizabeth hurried down off the stepladder, but when she got around to the other side of the tree, she found her son lost in concentration, meticulously trying to loop an ornament hook over a bow just too thick to take it.

Elizabeth was beginning to think she was hearing things when the sound came again:

Crunch! Crunch! Crunch!

She realized it was coming from outdoors.

She peeked out her front window, but the sun had slipped below the far hill, and the rosy glow it gave off was like an ember in the ashes that failed to give off either heat or warmth.

Crunch! Crunch!

There it was again.

Snuggling the neck of her cardigan around her throat, she opened the front door and called out a hello.

There was no response.

It was a cloudy night, and the dark beyond the door was a thick black curtain obscuring the view more than a few feet beyond the threshold.

Puzzled, Elizabeth closed the door.

In a short while the tree was decorated, and Timmy was beginning to nod off over a dessert of milk and Christmas cookies. He put up surprisingly little fuss about going to bed, although Elizabeth had to promise to wake him for a peek at Santa if she heard him come down the chimney.

Elizabeth had just closed Timmy's door when she was startled by a different noise downstairs. She felt a coldness in the pit of her stomach when she realized it was a voice.

Someone was downstairs.

How in god's name had they gotten in?

Tiptoeing to the landing, she craned her head around the corner and saw brighter light than could be cast by candles.

They had lights, and she was trapped upstairs in the dark!

The voice was sharply interrupted by a musical tone, and Linda found herself stifling a nervous laugh. It was the radio, which she remembered clicking on uselessly that morning at the height of the storm. In a moment she was downstairs, to discover that the power had come back on.

A news announcer was broadcasting the usual tales of Christmas cheer: reports of drunk drivers, a robbery at a department store, and the discovery of a sidewalk Santa who had been stabbed to death and relieved of his clothing. The announcer had just begun speaking about a police dragnet of some kind when Elizabeth spun the dial until she found Christmas carols.

In the front room, she had stood back from the tree to admire her and Timmy's handiwork when she heard the first noise again.

Crunch! Crunch!

It was coming from just the other side of the wall behind her.

She strode to the front door and opened it, looking down the path in the glare of the powerful porch light. She expected to see a public works truck parked in her yard, and a lineman coming up her walk. But all she saw was a trail of footprints gouging the snow in a single line leading up to the house from out of the darkness.

They had not been there when she had looked out an hour before.

Elizabeth quickly closed the door behind her and secured it with the double deadbolt.

Back in the kitchen, she fumbled for the telephone. It was still dead.

Had the wires been cut?

Crunch! Crunch!

She knew that the noises coming from the other side of the window were footsteps in the ice-crusted snow. She wanted to believe that a concerned neighbor had trekked to her house to find out if she was all right—or that a stranger stranded in the snow had managed to make his way to her house.

She turned around slowly. Then screamed.

A face was pressed against the window. The face of a monster. Icicles hung from its scraggly beard, and grime streaked deep creases into its face. An unholy light lit the thing's eyes, and it smiled a cruel toothy grin. It beckoned her gleefully with a darkly stained mitten.

It was hard for Elizabeth to acknowledge that the thing was actually a human being—a large maniacal gnome in a disheveled Santa costume.

It disappeared out of view toward the left of the window, and Elizabeth knew it was heading for the side door. She could hear it crunching through the snow, bumping off the side of the house.

Elizabeth rushed her way into the next room, knocking over a small pile of presents in her wake. She heard a fumbling at the lock and knew it wouldn't be long before the leering thing in the Santa suit made it through. Drawing on impossible reserves of strength, she hauled one of the freestanding cupboards before the door, its cups and saucers shattering as she dragged it across the floor.

She had just gotten her breath back when she heard the crunching footsteps advance to the other side of the door.

It was going on to try the next door!

Hysterical, Elizabeth stumbled into the next room, wrenching a chair from the table to jam forcefully under the doorknob.

And so it continued, with the thing outside forcing Elizabeth to follow its manic dance around the perimeter of the house. She had barely gotten a bookcase pulled in front of the dining room window before she heard the glass shattering and a thump on the back of the bookcase that nearly tipped it over.

Then for a moment the house was still. Elizabeth sat in the ruins of her downstairs, praying that Timmy not wake up, pleading silently for daylight.

Then she heard a clatter on the roof. And remembered the tree branch against the house that had taken out the phone line.

The chimney!

Elizabeth had laid a fire the night before in the log grate, but now she couldn't find a match anywhere. In horror, she saw soot and ashes flake down from inside the chimney.

Then she remembered the candles she had lit. She raced the first one over—but accidentally extinguished it in her haste.

The second one worked. The flames caught on the paper and kindling beneath the log and Elizabeth doused the fire with lighter fluid she had taken from the kitchen pantry. Flames jetted up the flue, and billowed a backdraft of smoke that left her coughing on the floor.

Half-sobbing, half-laughing, Elizabeth collapsed on the floor. The house was a shambles. But it was secure.

It was a moment before she saw the flames in the fireplace billow outward. Then she felt the draft. A blast of cool air was coming down the stairway from the upper rooms.

She hadn't even thought of the upstairs windows.

A squeal from Timmy was followed by the sound of heavy-soled boots clumping across the floor.

In horror, Elizabeth dragged herself to the bottom of the stairs and looked up.

Something large stood at the top, its upper half lost to the shadows that crowded the ceiling. Elizabeth could hear the dripping of ice and snow thawing off its clothing.

Timothy held its hand and began leading it down the stairs.

His face was beaming and he proudly declared his achievement:

Look, Mommy! I helped Santa get into our house for Christmas!

Yule Love Him

Sarah had forgotten all about her holiday dress until two days before Christmas. It had been tucked into a box that had mistakenly been grouped with the Christmas decorations instead of with the rest of her wardrobe.

She lifted it out of the box she had carried from the basement up to her front room, and watched it unfold to its full length. It was appropriately festive, a crosshatch pattern of red and green that might have looked plaid from a distance.

She vaguely remembered the last time she had worn it. It had been eight, maybe nine years before. A whole lifetime ago. She was living in the Midwest at the time. And she was dating Carl.

Her true love.

At least that was what she had thought as a twenty-one-year-old who had fallen head over heels for a fellow keyboarder at her first job out of school. She could still envision him, in his perpetual outfit of gray tweed jacket and jeans. Their relationship had begun with her teasing him that his clothing branded him as a terminal grad student.

The romance had been passionate—but brief, as most are at that age. The parting had not been amicable. Sarah owed her move to family back east—and a life that was different, if not better—in no small part to the heartbreak she had felt over their parting.

Over the years, she had fallen out of touch completely with the friends she and Carl had shared. It wasn't entirely unintentional, she knew; any more than her stowing the dress in a place she wouldn't think to look for it was.

Though she knew she was gambling with her self-esteem, she tried the dress on. The fabric felt unusually cold, but she attributed it to the coolness of the basement. To her surprise, the dress fit perfectly. The pleats fell perfectly, and the waste came in snugly, but not uncomfortably, as she had remembered.

Modeling it in front of her mirror, she decided she would wear it the next day. It would be her way of coming to terms with a past that still troubled her.

Sarah was up early on Christmas Eve to put the final touches on her decorations. Her family was due at midday, and she wanted to make a good impression. Despite her exertions cleaning and arranging, the dress still felt cold—almost damp. She thought possibly water had leaked onto it from her iron, but a quick inspection persuaded her it was just an unusual characteristic of the fabric.

She wondered if the strange sensation wasn't a sign she was coming down with something. All through her preparations, her skin had that numb, crawly feeling she sometimes felt when sickness was coming on. Several times she slapped at an imagined bug or spider on the back of her neck, until she realized the sensation was just part of her overall discomfort.

While making final adjustments to the drape of the dress, Sarah felt a sharp stab above her left breast. Pulling the neckline back for a peek, she saw the point of a safety pin protruding through the lining. No doubt it must have been dislodged by her earlier ironing.

Locating the rest of the pin, she worked it around to a hole and freed it from the stiff overlying brocade. It emerged with a wadded piece of paper attached.

Puzzled, Sarah unfolded the paper. Dessicated stems and leaves that had been ground to powder fell out of the pocket it had made. Sarah blew the dust off the paper and saw that it was a note—in Carl's hand.

With a stab of nostalgia, she remembered. Carl, the terminal grad student, had copied out a passage he had found in a book of holiday traditions their first Christmas together:

> *The lady who would bind to her affections forever the lover she has kissed beneath the mistletoe must sew a sprig from it into the breast of her corset.*

Corset? She and Carl had laughed over that! But he had given her the paper to wrap the spiky sprig in, and she had playfully pinned it in the lining of the dress.

The ringing of the doorbell interrupted Sarah's thoughts, and with a final tug she pulled the dress presentably into place. As she scrambled for the door, she noted an unusual smell in the foyer, and made a mental note to check the shoes in her closet and see if she had stepped in something.

With a flourish she opened the door, but her Merry Christmas! stopped in mid-cry.

She saw, to her total shock, that it was Carl.

No one had told her he had died—and so long ago.

Legend: If a woman kisses a man beneath the mistletoe on Christmas and sews a sprig into her corset, it will bind him to her forever as her true love.

O Christmas Tree!

Legend: A Christmas tree that proves impossible to decorate is discovered to have been grown in unhallowed soil.

Jeff Tyler gaped at the Christmas tree in disbelief. It was tilting to the side again!

He had adjusted the tree three times since putting it up the night before—manipulating the screws in the tree stand, planing the trunk, even cutting off boughs. Each time he made the tree look as perfectly set as he had before. Each time, he had come back into the room to find it listing to the left.

Jeff didn't understand it. The tree had looked perfectly balanced when he harvested it fresh from the Martindale Forest. It was the shape and height of the tree that had made it seem so appealing in the first place. Jeff couldn't believe that no one else had snatched it up, but he assumed most people in his neighborhood were content to buy trees precut from the local garden store.

The thing had been a nuisance since he'd picked it up. It had gouged a scar in the paint on top of his car as he'd tied it to the overhead luggage racks. Then, he could barely work it free when he got it home, and the thing nearly impaled him when repeated tugging finally pulled it down on top of him. This morning, Jeff had awakened with a horrible case of hives that were driving him mad with itching;

he knew that he'd gotten resin from the branches under his skin somehow putting the tree up the night before.

If Jeff hadn't known better, he'd almost have thought the tree didn't want to be a Christmas tree.

For a moment, he considered hacking the thing to tinder and stuffing it in the fireplace. Shimming the tree stand proved easier.

Trimming the tree was uneventful—at first. Jeff had gotten the tinsel and ornaments on to his satisfaction, and had only speared himself once with an ornament hook. He blamed his third mug of eggnog, not the tree, for his clumsiness.

Stringing the lights was more cumbersome. The tree was very full, and its branches proved nearly impenetrable. Jeff found it easier to stand on a stepladder to work the lights in than to reach his arms up from the ground.

Manipulating the electric wiring through dense branches forced Jeff's face close to the tree. As he peered between the tangle of branches, the darkness between them seemed to intensify. And expand. Jeff felt strange—almost as though he were being drawn inward toward the tree. He thought he saw shapes wriggling in the darkness, clarifying as they approached.

Jeff lurched backward, yelping as the stepladder tipped and he tumbled to the floor.

He had seen a face! An ancient bearded face! It had oozed from the darkness like sap from the tree bole. Its mouth had been open in a scream. And Jeff could feel there was something innately evil about it.

This is crazy, he thought.

But it took another mug of eggnog before his nerves felt steady enough to continue. No more faces materialized. By the time the job was done, Jeff was blaming what he'd seen on a combination of imagination and frustration at the tree's lack of cooperation.

Later that evening, shortly after he had retired to bed, Jeff heard singing. His alcohol-fogged mind assumed it was caroling; then he remembered that no one went around his neighborhood doing that.

Had he left the radio on?

Lying still in bed, he listened, trying to make out the melody. It was nothing he was familiar with—certainly nothing that matched the catalog of Christmas songs in his head. It wasn't a tune, really. Voices blended, but not in harmony. There was a rough, guttural quality to the indistinctly heard words. One voice keened to the height of a scream, weaving in and out of singing—no, not singing—chanting.

Jeff rose to get up from the bed and found that his T-shirt was sopping. Though he had turned the heat down before coming upstairs, he was sweating profusely. He shivered, but it seemed to be due to something other than the cool night air on his warm skin.

He tiptoed to the top of the stairway.

The eerie chanting was coming from the front room—where he'd put up the Christmas tree.

Slowly, he eased down the stairs. Three steps from the bottom, the oak planks groaned loudly. Jeff winced in apprehension. There was something in the house—he knew not what, but he didn't want his presence made known to it.

Inching his way toward the front room, he peered around the archway. . . .

The front room was a complete shambles. Furniture had been tipped over, and presents that he had placed beneath the tree only hours before were rudely tossed about, their wrapping torn from them. Some seemed not so much unwrapped as clawed open.

A strange smell pervaded the room, just powerful enough to override the piney scent of the tree. Jeff couldn't quite figure out what it was: a mix of dank, doggy-smelling fur and recently stifled matchsticks. Jeff was inspecting the lights for an exposed wire when he saw the imprints on the floor. Something had scuffed up furrows in the pile of the carpet at evenly spaced intervals. Jeff assumed they were footprints, and refused to call them what they really looked like:

Tracks.

He picked up the phone to report a burglary to the police, but stopped. As near he could tell, nothing had actually been taken. And a quick check of all the doors and windows yielded the puzzling discovery that all were still tightly locked up. No one had left the house—which meant no one had come in.

Jeff greeted his visiting family the next day in a sleepy fog. It had taken him the entire rest of the night to clean up the damage to the front room and try to repackage the salvageable gifts as best he could. He took ribbing from his brother about looking like the morning after a night of heavy Christmas cheer. And he endured jokes about the tilting tree, which he didn't even bother trying to fix anymore.

He was just hanging up coats when a child's scream sliced through the friendly holiday chatter. Jeff reached the front room at the same time as his brother and saw his four-year-old nephew, Timmy, cowering in the corner. Timmy had been the first guest to enter the front room and look for Christmas presents beneath the tree—and he had seen something that had nearly frightened him to death. He tried to put it into four-year-old words, but only his fear conveyed the certainty of the horrible thing he had witnessed.

An ornament lay crushed on the floor. Jeff saw that it was the decoration from the top of the tree: a singing angel holding open a book of songs, its starlike halo fanning out behind it. It had been pulverized almost to dust. Jeff's brother apologized for the mischief his protesting son had caused—but Jeff knew there was no way Timmy could have reached that ornament himself.

The situation returned to normal in a short time, although Jeff felt distracted and remote from events. He blamed it on his interrupted sleep the night before—but he also couldn't get the sound of that infernal chanting out of his head. He could swear he still heard it, and kept pumping up the volume of the Christmas carols on his stereo until his mother complained it was too loud for anyone to talk over.

When someone suggested a fire, Jeff welcomed the opportunity to concentrate on something else. He had laid logs and kindling in the fireplace the night before, and lighting them just a matter of opening the chimney flue and putting a match to the newspapers stuffed around the grate.

Jeff was concentrating on lighting the fire from several angles when he heard a collective shout of surprise behind him. Whipping his head around, he saw a completely unbelievable scene unfolding. The Christmas tree was somehow out of the tree stand and falling away from the fireplace!

Instinctively, Jeff dove to grab it and prevent it from falling on anyone. But he moved too slow. On the way down, the tree wrenched from the wall socket the wires and adapter that kept the lights blinking. Jeff heard the fizzle of a circuit shorting and smelled the ozoney aroma of sparks crackling in the air.

With a loud *Whuuummmp!* the tree ignited.

Jeff couldn't believe it. He had only cut the tree down three days before, but it flared like a piece of dry cardboard in a furnace. In seconds, the flames had spread to the gifts on the floor and the carpet.

Jeff's family scrambled for the front door. The sudden

draft of air its opening created fanned the fire to unbelievable intensity. Jeff helped Timmy through the doorway.
Then his luck ran out.

Years later, Timmy would tell his own family of the holiday tragedy that had claimed the life of his uncle, and the
inexplicable circumstances that he couldn't separate from
it. His uncle had cut down the tree in Martindale Forest, a
place that local Christmas tree sellers had traditionally
shunned. Martindale Forest was named for Josiah Martindale, who in 1675 had appointed himself Witchfinder General for the region of New England. Martindale had tried
only one case before dying mysteriously in his home, a
look of stark terror on his face. He had presided over the
sentencing of Naboth Price, an elderly man feared by his
neighbors to be guilty of the crime of trafficking with
Satan. Martindale had executed the man secretly on his
own land, on Christmas Day.

*It was rumored to be the only case in America of a witch
being burned at the stake.*

. . . In Small Packages

Legend: A Christmas present delivered to the wrong address contains a shocking surprise.

There was a funny smell in the front room. Ellen Beaumont noticed it early on Christmas Eve, in the midst of her final flurry of holiday preparations. It was a sourish smell that cut through the clean evergreen fragrance permeating the room from the Christmas tree.

Ellen quickly fanned her front door back and forth. It seemed to do the trick and she went back to her holiday baking. For a while she was caught up in the clouds of cinnamon, ginger, and nutmeg that spread their exotic character throughout the house. Only when the oven was off, and she stepped into the front room for relief from the kitchen heat, did she notice the smell again.

It was stronger this time, and more pungent. Ellen looked around the room, in every nook and cranny she could find. Had someone dropped food under the couch? Did a mouse die behind the home entertainment center? She couldn't quite place what was causing the odor, and it was beginning to annoy her. She didn't need distractions like this—not with all of her family due over in a couple of hours for their traditional Christmas celebration.

She called for her husband to take a break from his gift wrapping and come into the living room for a minute. Pete dropped a foil-wrapped present on top of the burgeoning stash beneath the tree and stood there sniffing. He confirmed that there was definitely a bad smell in the room—which made Ellen feel vindicated, since her overly sensitive nose had been a joke throughout their marriage. But he was darned if he could figure out what it was.

Sewage backup?

Ellen went into the kitchen and put her nose down near the drain.

Pete inspected the upstairs and downstairs bathrooms.

They both went down into the basement, expecting to see an oozing pipe somewhere. But their investigation turned up nothing. The basement actually smelled much better than the upstairs.

Ellen and Pete were completely stymied.

And the smell was getting more powerful. Worse, it was corrupting the more pleasant Christmas odors, making the sugar smells of the cookies and breads seem cloying and the piney Christmas tree smell rank and overfertilized.

Ellen began to worry about the furniture. If a smell like that were to get into the upholstery, it might never get out.

What was it?

Acting on a hunch, Ellen stood as close to the Christmas tree as the mound of gifts would let her. The bad odor was definitely coming from that corner. She performed a meticulous inspection of the tree, moving limb by limb, looking for an old bird's nest, a dead rodent, an insect egg case. Her efforts yielded nothing but a few itchy perforations of her fingertips where the blade-like fir needles cut into them.

The kids had strung popcorn and candy canes around the tree as they had done in years past. Could those turn rancid? No, it wasn't them.

Perhaps something had turned the water in the tree stand badly brackish. Ellen squatted down to floor level and stuck her fingers in. The cool water came out murky, but smelling only of wood and sap. It wasn't the source—but the smell was definitely close to the floor.

That's when Ellen realized that it had to be one of the gifts.

She couldn't believe it! There had to be close to forty gifts under the tree, some from her and Pete, some from the kids, some from traveling family who had sent them on ahead. Each one was wrapped in Christmas paper and bows and strategically placed beneath the tree.

Had one of their relatives done this as a practical joke?

Picking through the gifts at this point would completely disorganize them. Unwrapping gifts was out of the question—there would be no time left to rewrap them and Christmas would be spoiled.

Ellen called in the kids, then quizzed them and Pete. Had anyone bought something that could be making that smell? Something perishable?

No one would own up to it.

Ellen looked at her watch and was perturbed to see how much time she had wasted on this fruitless search. She broke out air freshener sticks, hiding them around the room, and asked Pete to stoke the fire with some peelings from the oranges she had used. If they couldn't eliminate the smell, they would at least try to combat it.

Family began arriving a short time later. The procession of people through the front door, and the fanning of the cold night air through the room, helped to diminish the smell's intensity at first. But once the door was closed and the heat of the numerous bodies made the room stuffier, it was hard not to notice. People began joking softly to one another, or scrutinizing dates brought by single family members, as though to ask, *Could that be them?*

Some of the more sensitive relatives retired to the kitchen, where the smell was the least noticeable.

Ellen eventually broke the news to the gathered crowd that she suspected someone in the room had sent a joke gift to the house. But the truth would be out, now that it was time to open presents.

The mystery of the smell's source lent an aura of expectancy to the revels. As each person opened a new gift, he or she grimaced or made some rude comment about what the box might contain. When Ellen and Pete opened a generic holiday gift pack of cheeses and smoked meats, they thought they had found the source of the smell. But a quick sniff test of the contents proved that the goods were still very well preserved.

The pile of gifts dwindled.

The noxious smell persisted.

By a quarter to one, the living-room floor was a sea of torn wrapping paper and unstrung ribbons. There was only one gift left to be opened.

Pete inspected it and found that there was no nametag on it.

He looked at Ellen. Ellen looked at him. Each flashed the other a quizzical expression that translated as *Don't know!*

It was a smallish box, perhaps a few inches on the side. Ellen had thought it might be jewelry.

No one in the room admitted to having sent it.

The wrapping paper had a snowman pattern on it that matched the pattern of one roll of paper Pete had used.

Then he remembered: a box had come in the mail perhaps a week and a half before. It was one of the first gifts to arrive, and Ellen had given it to him for wrapping. He assumed she had bought it. She assumed he had ordered it from a mail order catalog.

Regardless, the box had been wrapped and put under the tree, where it had sat all this time.

There was only one way to find out what was fouling the house with the smell, and Ellen volunteered to be the guinea pig. Her cousin passed the box to her, and everyone in the family watched intently as she unwrapped it.

When the flaps lifted up, the smell was worse, almost putrid. Ellen coughed, choking out to whoever was responsible that she didn't appreciate this. There was a smaller box inside. It had been white once, but had been turned yellow by whatever it contained. Ellen went to lift the lid, and the cardboard, which had turned spongy, collapsed in. There was just enough tension left in the lid to peel it back from the contents.

Ellen screamed—horribly!—and tossed the box to the floor. Everyone in the room saw what it contained: a good-sized hank of dirty blond hair and a black shriveled thing depending from it that oozed liquid on the carpet. Ellen's brother, a doctor, identified it as a human ear with a swatch of scalp attached. It had decomposed over the past week into a less than ideal specimen.

It was a gruesome denouement to the evening. It only got worse when Pete dug through the boxes put out with the garbage to find out what sick prankster was responsible. The box the "gift" had come in had no return address. It had been sent to a completely different state, but in the confusion of the holiday mail it had been misdelivered to Ellen and Pete.

Pete found a note mixed in with packing material in the box. It had been written with letters cut out of a magazine, the way he'd often seen criminals do it in movies. Horror gripped him as he read its terse message:

Pay me the ransom in 24 hours or the living part of your little girl gets buried alive!

Ħearth of Ħorror

Legend: Who hasn't heard the story of the chimney clogged since last Christmas, and what was found when it was cleaned out?

Jt was Christmas Eve, and Ted Lang was sitting at the dinner table with his family when he first became aware of the sounds coming from the wall in the living room.

Scratch . . . Scratch . . . Scratch . . .

At first Ted didn't even know he was hearing the noise. It was a subtle sound, easily lost against the background of clinking dinnerware, soft holiday music on the stereo, and animated conversation from his wife and children. But then one of those unpredictable silences occurred, and Ted not only heard the noise, but realized it had been weaving in and out of his hearing for a while.

Scratch . . . Scratch . . . Scratch . . .

Ted excused himself from the dinner table and went out front. The Christmas lights cast festive hues of red and green around the room. A pile of presents from family and friends were mounded under the tree, and it would be even bigger by morning, once Santa had come.

Ted listened intently for the noise but he heard nothing.

All in his imagination, he guessed.

Later that evening, however, as the family sat out front

celebrating with a yule log in the fireplace, Ted heard the sound again.

Scratch . . . Scratch . . . Scratch . . .

This time, everyone heard it. Even King, the family dog, who started pawing at the molding at the base of the wall.

Ted nudged King back with his foot. They had just paid good money to have their new east side brownstone refurbished and he wasn't about to let the dog ruin a costly decorating job.

Ted put his ear to the wall and listened. He heard a rustling sound behind the painted sheetrock. He turned to his wife and mouthed the same word he saw forming on her lips:

Mice.

But Ted was really thinking something else:

Rats!

Whatever was slithering through the walls of their house was bigger than the mice they occasionally spotted hurdling the tracks in the subway. Ted skittered his fingernails over the smooth wall to provoke a response.

WHUMP!

He nearly fell over an end table jumping back from the unexpected impact. He didn't want to think how big a paw a rodent would have to have to smack the wall that hard.

King barked fiercely, and Ted shushed him. It may have been Christmas Eve, but they still had the neighbors to think of.

When the kids asked him what he thought was making the noise, Ted told them he had heard somewhere that Santa sent reindeer scouts out to check and make sure all the children were in bed when he came to deliver their gifts. It took little prompting after that to get the kids tucked in snugly for the night.

By two in the morning, Ted had finished piling Santa's

gifts around the tree. Periodically, he cocked an ear toward the wall, listening for animal sound, but it appeared that the activity in the room had scared it off. He and his wife had turned in for bed when he remembered the milk and plate of cookies the kids had left out for Santa. Someone would have to put a dent in them before the kids catapulted out of bed that morning, or they'd be puzzled that Santa had refused their treat for him.

Ted was halfway down the stairs, loosely knotting his bathrobe belt, when he heard noises.

Rustle . . . Rustle . . . Rustle . . .

These were different from the sounds Ted had heard before. They were louder. And they were not being muffled by layers of plaster and mortar.

Someone was in the house.

Ted froze on the stairs leading down, his eyes accommodating slowly to the darkness. He didn't want to surprise a burglar. He knew the danger, and remembered reading somewhere that most burglars took the first thing they could carry and left without bothering anyone. But he was determined to protect the stairs—and his family.

Gradually, Ted made out the top of the tree. Its lights had been turned off, but the tinsel and ornaments caught light through the partly opened curtains and he was able to make out the tree's contours.

The rustle was coming from behind it.

Of course!

Someone was looking for valuables in the Christmas gifts.

Just last year, there had been news reports of a family that had gone to bed Christmas Eve and awakened to find that burglars had stolen into their house at night and taken all the gifts from under the tree.

Crunch!

A large present that had been tilted against another

shifted and fell over. It opened up a big space against the window, and Ted was just able to glimpse a silhouette, furtively rummaging next to the tree.

He couldn't believe what he was seeing.

It was a child!

The kid couldn't have been older than his own son or daughter. Had Ted not looked in on the kids seconds before coming back downstairs, he might have assumed one or the other of them was trying to sneak a peek at Santa.

How could a kid this young be breaking and entering a securely locked brownstone in the wee hours of Christmas morning?

At that moment, a floorboard chose to groan under the weight of Ted's foot.

The figure crouching at the tree jerked its head up, then sprinted across the room. It was almost to the far wall when Ted tackled it.

Ted wrestled with the small form, but no matter how hard he grappled with it the child kept slipping from his grasp. There was an oily feel to his skin and clothes, like graphite.

In the scuffle Ted managed to claw his fingers into the child's hair. The palm of his hand connected with skin, but where Ted expected to feel the soft downy skin of a child, he felt something cold and smooth, like the leather on a football. The feeling was unexpectedly repulsive. Ted's face was near the child's, and suddenly there was an exhalation of air smelling of soot and tar and something even more revolting.

Ted's fingers loosened as he coughed against the nauseating stink.

The child used that moment to break free of his grasp and run headlong for the wall.

Ted waited for the thud of flesh against an unyielding

surface. To his horrified disbelief, the boy appeared to pen-
etrate the wall like a knife blade slicing through water.

Bile rising in his throat, Ted sputtered and coughed his
way over to the light switch. The gifts had been knocked
from their tidy piles. And the spot where he had struggled
with the boy was blackened with a coarse, gritty dirt that
Ted knew must be covering him as well. He could tell from
the reek that it was soot and ash—which made absolutely
no sense, since the fireplace was on the other side of the
room and did not appear to have been disturbed.

The foul-smelling black material smudged the wall
where Ted had last seen the boy—the same wall where he
had heard the rats running earlier that evening! Stepping
up to it, Ted made a series of taps across the surface. In the
silence of the midwinter night, he picked up the subtle
change in tone of his knocks. Part of the wall seemed solid
as stone, but there was a hollow spot midway over and
down.

Stepping back from the wall, Ted kicked something with
the toes of his bare foot. Pressed into the soiled pile of the
carpet where he had been wrestling with the intruder only
moments before was a small, soot-covered ornament: a
beautifully painted figurine of a young girl dressed in winter garb from the nineteenth century. Ted had never seen
it before, and didn't recall his wife ever having bought it.
The figure appeared to be made of some durable ceramic—but a nearby antiques store established later that it
was sculpted ivory with solid gold inlay, a genuine antique
of the Victorian era that would have been worth even more
if Ted had also produced the accompanying male figure.

The rest of the sad story we owe to the history department of the city university, which was consulted when
workmen explored the wall where Ted's family had heard
the rat noises. It was not uncommon for houses like Ted's

to have been built with a second chimney, and even less uncommon for a modern dwelling to have all but one chimney sealed up. The nineteenth century had been a flush time for chimney sweeps, and the chimney sweep business had been as unscrupulous as it was heartless. Master sweeps frequently used the smallest of the orphan boys in their employ to shimmy into crevices no adult sweep could clean. Sometimes they tasked these boys with sneaking into rich households at holiday time and stealing valuables, which were frequently in full view around the Christmas tree.

How else to explain the century-old remains of a tiny boy in chimney sweep garb found trapped in the bricked-over chimney—or the tiny ivory figurine of a boy in Victorian dress found clenched in one of its skeletal hands?

ฅalloween
ฅorrors

Is there any holiday more appropriate for the telling of horror stories than Halloween? Although we think of October 31 as a day given over more to imagined than real horrors, Halloween comes with a long pedigree of supernatural associations. Supposedly piggybacked on a pagan day of celebration, the day we call Halloween was formally known as All Hallows' Eve, an interval marked by mischief and mayhem that must inevitably give way to the sanctity of All Hallows on November 1—also known as All Saints Day.

It's worth noting that in some places, this balance of wickedness and goodness extends on either side of the holiday. In many parts of America, October 30 is acknowledged as "Mischief Night," when the same children who come to your door on Halloween asking for candy have license to soap windows and commit other devilish acts. In many countries around the world, November 2 is All Souls Day, a feast day for the souls of the faithful departed that is celebrated with joyous, sometimes comic evocations of death.

Even in secular society Halloween has its dark connotations. It comes on the last day of October and thus marks the end of the harvest season. Its many traditional symbols—among them the scarecrow and the pumpkin carved into a jack-o'-lantern—are thus associated with the death of the year. Add to this the fact that the fall season Halloween commemorates is marked by increasingly shorter days and longer nights. Traditionally, the forces of supernatural evil flourished in darkness, and thus we add their emblems—the witch, the black cat, the spirit or ghost, the vampire, the skeleton, the goblin—to the menagerie of Halloween beings. The ritual of trick-or-treating, where candy and sweets are given to children who masquerade as these malevolent creatures, is based on the belief that placating supernatural menaces is a way of preventing misfortune from befalling one's household.

Of course Halloween is celebrated all in the spirit of fun. But that hasn't prevented a host of modern superstitions and legends from accreting around it. There are reports (so we've heard) of trick-or-treaters who found out afterward that they could not remove their costumes and were forever the monsters they dressed up as. Similarly, there have been any number of deaths of homeowners who opened their door to the figure of the Grim Reaper on Halloween, unaware that it really was Death come to claim their souls. (We know this from the very "scientific" evidence of a cowled skeletal face left imprinted on their retinas at the time of death.) Real-life incidents of adulterated Halloween candy result every year in accounts of Halloween poisonings or the discovery of chopped-up body parts doled out anonymously into Halloween bags.

The popularity of scores of Hollywood movies in which genuinely nasty horrors make their way under the cover of Halloween make-believe has helped to spawn its share of Halloween tall tales. Every so often, we hear the story of the famous psychic who predicts that a mass murder will occur on a college campus. Any student at these bastions of enlightenment who dismisses the warning as nonsense risks getting stabbed by a costumed, maniacal fellow student or professor who believes he or she must kill thirteen people as part of some unorthodox ritual. Women's colleges and schools whose colors are orange and black are particularly vulnerable.

With so much madness regularly afoot on the night of October 31, it's inevitable that someone will really push luck and openly invite danger. Some readers are no doubt aware of the young woman who followed through on a dare to spend Halloween night by herself in a graveyard and was found dead the next day in the arms of the statue of an angel perched atop a mausoleum—twenty feet off the ground!

What this all adds up to is that Halloween is a night when only the young and innocent or the foolhardy and malicious are about. The sane person will stay inside behind locked doors and enjoy the holiday vicariously by reading Halloween horror stories.

It's a safe diversion.

Isn't it?

Tricks and Treats

Legend: *On Halloween night, a parent discovers that what he thinks is a trick-or-treater masquerading as a ghost is a real ghost.*

It was just past dusk when Mark Hansom first saw the little boy. The kid was standing across the street, inside the vacant lot next to the Ryan house.

Mark had pulled trick-or-treat watch duty this Halloween. He was busy keeping an eye on his own two boys and the group of friends they were walking with. He wouldn't have noticed the kid but for the fact that he was all by himself. Parents rarely let their kids go out trick-or-treating alone these days. It was a sad commentary on the times that there were sick people out there who took advantage of Halloween to prey on little kids.

The boy just stood there holding his goodie sack before him. It looked like he'd made a pretty good haul already. He was holding each handle with one hand, and the bag dipped heavily toward the ground.

Why was he standing in the lot and not walking up and down the street?

Mark saw other groups of kids pass by in either direction on the kid's side of the street. No one seemed to pay any attention to him. The boy had probably run ahead of a group or his parents. No doubt, they'd catch up with him shortly.

Mark's thoughts were interrupted by the calls of his kids, who knew better than to get too far ahead of their old man. Deciding that there were limits to his responsibilities, he followed his boys and their buddies up the street.

It was a splendid Halloween night. A full moon was up, slipping in and out of wispy cloud patches like a bloated spider through its web. Leaves dusted the sidewalks and made a crisp crackling noise as the kids swept by. There was just a touch of chill. If that didn't put a person in mind of the dying year, then the rich, loamy smell of decaying plants and damp, moldy forest would.

Mark was so caught up in his thoughts of the season that he almost missed the boy on his way up the street. He hadn't really been expecting to see him, and wasn't even thinking to look for him. But there he was, perhaps ten paces into the vacant lot, holding the same posture Mark had seen him keep before: feet planted, bag out front, hands tightly bearing up their burden.

From this side of the street Mark could just make out the kid's costume: a skeleton. Pretty common outfit a few years back, but a bit outdated now, Mark thought, surveying the array of cartoon and movie character getups most of the kids were wearing.

The kid's outfit was just discernible against the darkness of the lot, even though the moon was behind a cloud. Mark guessed that the costume was painted with that glow-in-the-dark paint that was supposed to make it look even spookier at night. He had to admit, the glow the kid was giving off made him look pretty eerie.

Though his own kids were dressed up like television action figures, he gave credit to the trick-or-treaters who disguised themselves as something scary. It seemed more appropriate for the day.

But the kid was just standing there. All alone, like before.

In fact, Mark wondered if he had even changed his position.

An empty lot was no place for a kid to be playing, especially at night. There were too many things he could get hurt on: tree stumps, holes, rocks, broken glass. On Halloween night, kids usually had their minds on other things besides their own safety, and their costumes sometimes hid things from sight they should be paying attention to.

Hey!

Mark called out to the boy. But got no response.

With a shrug of his shoulders, Mark went back to the duties he'd agreed to for the night. His kids and their friends were enough of a handful.

By ten o'clock, trick-or-treating was over and the house lights were down to the feeble glow of an old monster movie running on television sets in the front rooms. Mark was trying to relax with a Boris Karloff film while his kids counted out and traded their evening's stash, but he couldn't get his mind off that kid in the lot. He knew if he didn't at least check back he wouldn't be able to sleep that evening, so he made an excuse to his wife about having to go out and get a can of coffee for the morning and set off on foot.

The neighborhood was a sharp contrast to what it had been only half an hour before: quiet, almost dead. Mark thought the echo of his footsteps was the loneliest sound he had ever heard. He rounded the corner and saw two kids about his boys' height coming toward him. He hoped that one of them might be the kid in the lot, picked up by a friend or brother, but neither of the two was wearing a skeleton costume.

Then, he was in front of the lot.

And the kid was still standing there.

Mark could have sworn that he hadn't moved an inch since he'd first seen him hours ago. That wasn't like any kid he could think of. Something had to be wrong.

Hey, kid!

Mark called out to the boy. There was no movement. Mark beckoned vigorously with his hand, but the kid was definitely off in another world.

With a sigh, Mark stepped into the field. Almost immediately, he drew his overcoat taut around him. It felt like there had been a temperature drop of several degrees in a single pace. A breeze sprang up, and Mark was glad to blame it on that.

The moon was still slipping in and out of the clouds, and the light patterns it threw on the furrowed ground were creepy. Black turned to silver, and gave the hummocks and divots a pale, otherworldly look, before turning black again.

The wind whipped up as he closed in on the kid and called to him again, asking if he was okay. Mark felt a growing sense of discomfort, as much from the kid's silence as from the realization that though his own coat was whipping in the wind the kid's outfit wasn't even ruffling.

Mark asked the boy if he was lost, if he knew where he lived. He was within a foot of the kid and he squatted down to make eye contact so that he wouldn't seem intimidating. Close to the ground, he could smell the overripe aroma of rot. Something in the landscape was putrid, and Mark only hoped he hadn't stepped in it.

The kid's mask was quite effective. What had appeared a simple skull face from the sidewalk was one of the more gruesome death masks he'd seen, with clumps of hair and strings of flesh hanging from it. In the flickering moonlight Mark made out a huge bloody cut that extended all the way around the neck. He couldn't recall ever having seen this outfit for sale in the stores, and was surprised they were actually marketing something so gory to youngsters.

Suddenly, he realized what the kid was doing. He wasn't just hefting the bulging bag. He was holding it out for someone to look into. But for several hours? Was this some kind of game?

You want me to look into the bag? Mark asked, looking down, just as the moon sailed out from behind a cloud and lit the landscape deathly white.

Mark screamed.

In fact, it was his scream that brought the neighbors running from their houses. They couldn't get Mark to leave the lot without calling the police. Mark was so persuasive in his story about a little kid with a trick-or-treat bag that they decided to investigate.

The following day, the police were able to finally close the files on Jimmy Christopher, a little boy who had gone out trick-or-treating around the neighborhood ten years before and never come home. It was Jimmy's disappearance that had convinced most parents from that day on not to let their kids go out on Halloween by themselves.

The cops had found Jimmy's mutilated body within a week of his disappearance.

But it wasn't until they dug in the lot, at the spot Mark showed them, that they found his missing head.

ꟿasquerade

Al Blackwood felt stifled in his Halloween costume.
He couldn't figure out why. It was just a mourning suit: solemn dark homespun, starched white shirt, and a string tie that gave him a sort of nineteenth-century look. The fit was a little tight, but not so tight that he should feel this uncomfortable.

He had hoped a cold beer would bring relief, but it only seemed to make him feel worse. Like he was suffocating.

He couldn't wait to leave the party.

He had decided to dress up like a zombie only after coming across the outfit in an undervisited corner of the costume store. The proprietor had assured him it was the genuine article: authentic nineteenth-century mortuary garb, the kind of suit they planted folks in back then guaranteed to make him look like he'd risen from the grave.

Al daubed at trickles of sweat running down his face, trying not to smudge the white pancake makeup and eyeshadow he'd used to give himself that dead-alive look. The cloth of the suit was not absorbing any of the liquid. It didn't surprise him in the least. He'd known upon picking the suit up that it had been treated with powerful chemicals. There was an aroma of something pungent and alcoholic in that corner of the costume shop, and at first Al had suspected the proprietor was tippling in the back. Then he realized the smell was coming from the suit.

The thing must have been bombed with some sort of super-mothball. It seemed to have worked. The fabric was in beautiful shape, and there had actually been several moth carcasses on the floor under the rack it hung on.

The proprietor had convinced Al the smell would dissipate once it was taken outdoors. He'd also dropped the price a few bucks.

Al stared in envy at the people parading past him dressed as vampires and werewolves. Even the tightly wrapped mummies were having more fun than he was.

The first wave of wooziness hit him as he pushed away from the bar. He felt light-headed and fuzzy. Al looked down at the drink in his hand, but he knew it wasn't just the alcohol making him feel this way.

He needed fresh air—but the door to the patio looked unusually far away, like he was seeing it through the wrong end of a telescope. The path to it was an obstacle course of loud partyers he wasn't up to dealing with.

He sought out the bedroom behind him. It was only a few steps away, but it seemed to take forever to reach it. His legs had become leaden, and every step took herculean strength.

He knew he had to get off his feet, and his body obliged, plunging him down into a bottomless pit that he knew was really only a drop of about three feet onto the bed.

Al folded his hands over his chest and closed his eyes, praying for the weird feeling to pass.

It didn't.

He felt a tingling on his back, where the costume was pressing into his skin. The tingling turned to a dull warmth, then fiery discomfort.

He tried to lift himself up, but couldn't.

The lights of the room were dimming—but he knew the lamp next to the bed was shining brightly.

He turned his head with great effort toward the door, saw partyers passing by—but he could hear no sound.

The irritation of the suit was giving way to a numb feeling.

He couldn't move.

He sensed nothing.

He felt as though he'd been buried alive inside his own body.

They found Al when the party broke up at 3 A.M. His body lay in perfect repose, with hands neatly crossed and face pointing straight up toward the ceiling.

In the mourning suit, he looked like a perfectly dressed corpse. And he was.

The medical examiner's report on the cause of death made no sense whatsoever—until Al's outfit was traced back to the costume store. The proprietor told the police the same thing he had told Al, about the mourning suit's authenticity.

It didn't make a lot of sense to the cops, but it did to the mortician who prepared Al for burial. A century ago, mortuary science was much cruder and techniques of preservation more primitive. It wasn't uncommon to completely impregnate a corpse with preservatives so that it would stay intact during the mourning period. There were reports of mourners being overcome by the volatile chemical fumes in houses where a dressed corpse was being viewed.

The fabric of Al's corpse costume was completely saturated with embalming fluid.

And within hours of donning it, so was Al.

Legend: A costume turns out to be actual clothes used by morticians to dress a corpse. It has absorbed so much embalming fluid that it kills the person who wears it.

Scarecrow

Legend: Halloween decorations are actually secret talismans that warn evil spirits away from the houses that have them.

Mitch and Jean Kelly moved to their new neighborhood a week before Halloween. Almost immediately, they noticed the scarecrows.

Not real scarecrows—decorative ones. Most were about three feet tall, decked out in overalls and flannel shirts, with painted smiles flashing beneath rumpled felt hats. Many were parts of displays that included a pumpkin and a harvest sheaf. Others stood alone. Some were simply doll-sized figures of dried silk twisted out of cornhusks and propped conspicuously in a window. But every house had one—except theirs.

Mitch guessed that this was the average suburbanite's idea of "quaint." He thought the things looked damned ugly. Put one up in front of your house and it was like putting out a vacancy sign for bugs, spiders, and anything else that liked to crawl indoors.

It made no sense to Mitch why a town that couldn't claim to have a single field or pasture would so obsessively display a prop everyone associated with farm life. Didn't people know scarecrows were created to scare animals away from the crops? What point was there to putting one up as a decoration in an upper-middle-class neighborhood where the closest anyone got to farming was the produce section of the local supermarket?

Clearly, there was a lot Mitch and Jean were going to have to get used to about their new home. Already, they felt like outsiders. Just three days before they had been shopping at the local market for a pumpkin. It had been their tradition for as long as they had been married to carve a jack-o'-lantern the day before Halloween and put it on their front porch. On Halloween night, the lit jack-o'-lantern served as a beacon to trick-or-treaters. But the only pumpkins to be found at the local supermarket were parts of scarecrow displays. Mitch had removed one and brought it up to the cash register but was told the store wouldn't sell it as a solitary item. He had argued, but the clerk remained adamant. Finally, Mitch told the clerk angrily to charge him for the whole damn display and to stuff the scarecrow wherever he wanted.

Mitch felt good about having stood up for his principles, even though it had cost him fifty bucks.

The clerk had told him on his way out that he might as well take the scarecrow, since he'd paid for it.

Over my dead body, Mitch had muttered.

That Saturday, Mitch and Jean carved their jack-o'-lantern, but by sundown that evening pieces of it were clotted on the front door. Someone had hurled it at their house! Mitch called the police department to protest the vandalism. The police officer he reached gave him a song and dance about mischief night, and kids beings kids, and how it wasn't likely they could catch the culprit if Mitch hadn't actually seen him do it.

Mitch would not be deterred. On Halloween morning he drove to a store the next town over and bought an even bigger pumpkin. It was carved, lit, and out front, under Mitch's watchful eye, by noon that day.

The evening came on fast and showed all signs of being

a perfect Halloween night. The sun had turned the distant hills a fiery red as it set. In its wake, the moon had risen with a pinkish glow that Mitch knew made it what they called a blood moon. The air was just cool enough to sharpen smells and sounds. Mitch picked up the acrid waft of burning wood that told him several fireplaces were being stoked nearby.

He had stocked up on candy for the neighborhood kids. Jean had wistfully suggested that they might get to meet some of the neighbors whose kids came trick-or-treating. By dusk they had already seen some kids out in costume traipsing around the block. But none came to their door. Mitch peeked through their blinds and saw one cluster of kids at the house next door. He waited for the ring of their doorbell—but it never came. After several minutes he peeked back outside again, and saw the kids heading up the steps at the house on the other side.

Their house had been completely skipped over.

It went on like that the rest of the evening.

The neighborhood kids were out in droves, in costumes ranging from the store-bought to the crudely homemade. They laughed and yelled as they paraded up and down the street. But in every case they passed by the Kelly house like they didn't even see it there.

Mitch and Jean had come close to getting only one visitor that evening. Early on, Mitch had seen one kid who couldn't have been more than three or four come toddling up the front walk in a ghost sheet. Mitch had stepped into the foyer, planning to open the door as the child came up the steps. But through the glass panes at the top of the door, he saw a woman—probably the kid's mother—run to the child and yank him away by the arm before he could even get halfway up the walk.

What the hell was everyone's problem?

Mitch guessed the kids were just going to the houses of

friends and people they knew. It was probably a good safety precaution these days.

By ten o'clock not a single trick-or-treater had come to their door. Mitch had offered to answer the doorbell while Jean worked upstairs, but it seemed pretty pointless. The cries of the kids and the pounding of feet on the sidewalk had just ceased suddenly. Mitch looked through the front window and saw that the block was completely dark. The neighbors were either sending a signal to the kids that Halloween was over, or they were turning in much earlier than usual.

Mitch was just preparing to go out and extinguish the light in the jack-o'-lantern when he was startled by a sound from the front porch.

Whummmp!

The stillness of the night had magnified the noise. It sounded like something had fallen to the floorboards. Opening the door, Mitch discovered another jack-o'-lantern casualty. Someone had tossed it, candle and all, against the front door. This was worse than the one yesterday. The pumpkin was virtually pulverized. Stringy clumps spattered the door, and flecks of pumpkin dressed the walls several feet on either side of the frame.

It would have taken considerable strength to make that kind of mess. No little kid out for Halloween could have done this.

Mitch stood in the doorway, peering into the darkness as though he might see whoever was responsible for this prank. The candle in the jack-o'-lantern had been smothered by soppy pulp, and he could smell that smoky, oily smell that he associated with a snuffed candle. But there was another, stronger smell behind it. A sweet-and-sour smell. It reminded him of that mixed aroma of alfalfa, manure, and newly turned earth that he associated with the country. As a kid, he remembered how overpowering it could seem whenever he drove by a recently mown hayfield. It was the first time he'd ever smelled it in this town.

What was putting that smell out so strongly?

Hey!

Mitch yelled into inky darkness, hoping to scare off whoever had tossed the pumpkin. A light breeze made the treetops dance in the moonlight. Mitch heard a slithering rustle.

Must be leaves.

But he knew that all the leaves had been off the trees a week ago. And that they had raked the last of them out of their yard before the weekend.

The wind made the rustling sound again, and Mitch felt the hairs on his arms prickle.

Rubbing them against the chill, he stepped back indoors. He had just picked up the phone to call the police and complain a second time when he heard the rustling noise again.

Sssssssssssssss . . .

It was coming from the front porch.

Sssssssssssssss . . .

Much closer than it had been before.

It was followed by a clumping sound. Like something hitting the floorboards at regular intervals.

Pok . . . Pok . . . Pok.

Mitch turned out the lights.

On tiptoe, he advanced toward the front window.

Sssssssssssssss . . .

Whatever it was, it was being dragged across the front screens.

Sticking his fingers between the slats of the blinds, he peered out.

Nothing there.

Sssssssssssssss . . .

It brushed over the screen on the window near the door.

Someone was going to a lot of effort to put a Halloween scare into him.

Pok . . . Pok . . . Pok.

It sounded like footsteps outside the front door. Or someone tapping the porch with a pole.

Mitch moved silently to the foyer and peeked through the panes of the window.

Someone was standing on the porch. Mitch could just make out an overcoat and a slouch hat on the head. The person was carrying a walking stick in his hand, thumping it on the porch planking.

A late trick-or-treater?

Mitch clicked the light on as he pulled the door open. He was almost driven back by the smell he had noticed before. Now it was ten times stronger and nauseatingly potent. Concentrated, it reminded him less of wet straw and more of the stench of decay and death.

The person on the porch was dressed like a scarecrow, with shocks of loose straw sticking out around his wrists and neck. He turned his face up to look directly at Mitch.

And Mitch realized that the figure was not wearing a costume.

Black holes marked where its eyes should be. Its mouth was stitched shut, but Mitch could have sworn the cheeks worked behind it, huffing and puffing as though it were alive. What Mitch had at first thought was a nose was actually a field spider the size of his hand. Other things he couldn't quite see wriggled in the straw jutting out beneath the figure's hat.

The scarecrow took a step forward and Mitch saw that what he had mistaken for a walking stick was a weathered wood stave. It had a crossbar at the top. Its other end was a pointy stake.

The thing moved fast.

Mitch never had a chance. Neither did Jean.

The next day, the neighbors saw two scarecrows up on poles at the new peoples' house. They didn't look like the other scarecrows around the neighborhood. They wore Mitch and Jean's clothes. And they weren't stuffed with straw.

But everyone agreed from the way they flapped loosely in the wind that they did a good job of scaring things away.

Sweets to the Sweet

Legend: Trick-or-treaters discover that some house along their route has been dropping body parts into their bags.

hop! Chop! Chop!

C   Esther Charles was preparing ingredients for her Halloween goodies.

Halloween was Esther's favorite day of the year. It had been since she was a little girl. This year, she was going all out in her efforts.

Slice! Slice! Slice!

It had been a long time since she had been able to apply herself so to the making of Halloween treats. So long that she had heard people didn't make their own candies and confections anymore for the special day. Worse, children were actually told by their parents *not to eat* homemade Halloween candies.

The idea!

Grind! Grind! Grind!

Esther couldn't imagine Halloween treats without the homemade touch: sugary bites that crunched between the teeth, delicate drops that popped their juices when bitten, creamy filled chocolates with deliciously oozy centers. She had everything she needed to make them all. And she would!

Though it had been some time, Esther still remembered her favorite recipes by heart.

Sift! Sift! Sift!

Many of the ingredients she had picked up the day before in the local grocery store.

Flours that incorporated runny liquids.

Creams that bound crunchies in secret suspensions.

Sweeteners that absorbed extracts, essences, and dyes.

Some of the special ingredients had to be improvised, but the basics never changed.

Drip! Drip! Drip!

Other things never changed too. Things that Esther wished just as soon would. The unthinking cruelty of children was the worst.

Bubble! Bubble! Bubble!

Just yesterday in the grocery store she had heard them snickering to one another in the aisle behind her. When she turned upon them, they had made nasty faces at her. Faces so nasty that she wanted to tell them they didn't need Halloween masks!

Scrape! Scrape! Scrape!

The worst had been that wicked little boy she had surprised outside her home in the midst of his mischief that same evening. She knew that many children flaunted their misbehavior around the neighborhood the night before Halloween, but just because it was expected didn't make it right. She had caught him red-handed writing words in soap on her windows.

Vicious words. Unkind words. Untrue words.

Witch.

Mad.

Murderer.

Pull! Pull! Pull!

And when she confronted him, he had the nerve to taunt her! He had said everyone knew about her, and what she had done, and why they had put her away in that place of sickness for so long, and how everyone was afraid of her.

She had quickly put a stop to his lies.

Grate! Grate! Grate!

Ellen ran a flour-caked hand through her stringy hair. She could tell from the way the sun dipped over the hills that she still had a couple of hours of daylight left. Just enough time for her goodies to cool and set before wrapping.

Esther stepped back from the table to survey her handiwork.

It was nice to see how her work had become second nature to her.

Pat! Pat! Pat!

She would not let unpleasant children spoil her favorite holiday. She would give them her special Halloween candies—*and* a taste of their own medicine!

As Esther set about the final steps that would give added surprise to her Halloween treats, she stifled a giggle over something she had overheard at the store yesterday.

When she had taken her purchases to the checkout counter, a sweet little girl had looked at the cellophane packages of candy corn and told her mother how they looked just like teeth.

Studying her ingredients, Esther knew that, really, it was the other way around.

Bloody Mary

Legend: If you stand in a darkened room before a mirror and chant the name of the witch Bloody Mary, the face of the devil will appear in the mirror.

It all began as a dare, remember. A silly challenge, the kind my kid brother makes to his grade school buddies. You know, like, *C'mon scaredy cat—double dare you to press the old witch's doorbell.*

We could have spent the evening like Halloweens past—playing dumb pranks on one another, drinking till we got sick and blaming it on the candy we ate, necking in the bedrooms upstairs, not doing all those forbidden things we would brag next day we had done. But you wouldn't have been happy with that. Not at your parents' house. Not at *your* Halloween party.

When the last of the cheesy horror videos ran out on the VCR, and it was clear we had nothing to say to one another that hadn't been said at school that day, you suggested something new and different. You got out that book of spooky folk legends you had bought at the mall. Maybe we could spook ourselves reading them aloud.

Bravo! What imagination!

So we all sat around reading about the vanishing hitch-hiker, the psychopath hiding in the closet, and Cropsey the headsman, acting like we were really scared by all this nonsense.

When the book circled around to you, you read your favorite, the legend of Bloody Mary:

Bloody Mary was a seventeenth-century witch woman who sold her soul to the devil for supernatural powers. Every Halloween, until she was caught and burned at the stake, she renewed her pact by sacrificing an infant from her village before a mirror, where the face of the devil would appear. At midnight on Halloween, if you sit alone before a mirror in a darkened room, with only a candle for light, and say the name Bloody Mary five times in succession, you'll see the face of the devil.

No one said anything as you slowly closed the book. Everyone was thinking the same thing. Was it just coincidence that you had given your little performance at a quarter to midnight on Bloody Mary's night?

The only problem was, no one wanted to try it. Of course, we all joked about what a stupid superstition it was. The story made no sense. It was so pointless there was no reason to try it out. A little ridicule goes a long way toward propping up the weak struts of one's courage, doesn't it?

If I hadn't snorted the loudest, perhaps you all would have dared someone else. But I was never one to keep my feelings inside, and I had already had enough of the cider—and whatever you had spiked it with—to lower my resistance. Besides, as you all bravely assured me, if the story was really so unbelievable, there was nothing to worry about. Right?

So we all trotted up to your parents' bedroom. It wasn't the only room in the house with a mirror, but you certainly didn't want anything of this sort being tried with *your* mirror, the one you fawned over yourself in every day, did you?

I took the black wax candle you had bought for decoration and solemnly swore, as I closed the door, that I would wait until the church bell began tolling midnight to say what I had to, and that I would say it loud enough for you all to hear.

There's not much more to tell you that you don't already know—is there? With the candle lighting my face from beneath my chin and making it look like a gaunt trick-or-treat mask, I fixed my eyes on the mirror. When the first stroke of midnight struck, I said *Bloody Mary*.

It came out as a croak that could barely be heard, so I swallowed and said it again.

Bloody Mary.

My eyes didn't even blink. The next time, I said it louder.

Bloody Mary!

Maybe it was my imagination, but the candle seemed to flicker a bit, hollowing the look of my eyes into dark pools, as I said it a fourth time.

Bloody Mary!

I waited just a moment then. I wanted to tease you all so that you might feel just a bit of the apprehension I felt, all by myself following through on a fool's bet in that dark room. I wanted you to wonder if my nerves would fail. So I waited until the final stroke of midnight, before blurting it out:

BLOODY MARY!

I don't know what I was expecting: A puff of smoke, the smell of brimstone, the operatic howls of the minions of hell. But there was nothing so dramatic. Just the all-too-honest reflecting surface of the polished glass before me.

Outside, in the hallway, someone screamed—solely for effect, it seems. All the rest of you giggled obnoxiously in relief.

It must have been about a minute before one of you called out my name. Perhaps another half minute before someone pounded on the door. None of my greatly concerned friends believed the legend any more than I did. But no one wanted to be the first person to open the door. Did they?

When I flung it wide, you should have seen the startled looks on your faces. Like a bunch of trick-or-treaters who had seen a *real* ghost. It didn't take much persuasion to convince you that the experience had been an abysmal bore. And that now it was time to get on with the real partying.

I killed the first of you an hour later. It was appallingly easy. Add the element of surprise to a little pressure from the thumbs and the average windpipe crushes like a paper cup.

I continued on, room to room, showing you all just how easy it was. Some of you had to be lulled first with the stupid small talk that passes as important conversation between yourselves. Others were so disabled by the night's festivities it almost didn't seem fair to take advantage.

But it didn't take much to get each of you alone. And in the final moments I showed each of you just how vulnerable you were, how dreadful the horrors of Halloween night could be.

The last one was your sister. I found her in her room. I used her pillow. Can you imagine what must have been going through her mind as she struggled beneath the very cushion she had comfortably gone to sleep on every night for all these years?

Pleasant dreams, I whispered to her.

And now it's your turn.

You're the only one left, and I know you're here, somewhere. Maybe you're in the back of one of the closets, whimpering a prayer that I won't find you. Maybe you've holed up in some secret hiding place you've known about since childhood and are damning me to hell, hoping I'll grow tired of this game we're playing and just leave you alone.

This *is* a big house. But I am very thorough.

You've been very patient as I've gone around blocking the doors behind me and wedging the windows shut. I didn't hear a peep out of you, even though you must have known that each scrape of wood, each rattle of metal meant another escape route closed off. Maybe you've accepted that there is *no* escape. And that what's going to happen is as inevitable as—well, as inevitable as Halloween giving way to All Saints Day.

Because you've been such a good sport about this, I'm going to tell you something. Something none of the others knew, though they might have had an inkling in their last lucid moment.

When my hands close around your throat, and the lights start to dim, I want you look me in the eyes. Then you'll know what I discovered sitting by myself in that room, staring innocently in that revealing mirror:

You don't need a candle.

You don't need a mirror.

You don't even need to chant, Bloody Mary.

Look straight at *me,* and do you know what you'll see?

You'll see the face of the devil.